Argument Against
the Good-Looking Corpse

~~Charles Alcorn~~

Texas Review Press
Huntsville, Texas

FIRST EDITION, 2011

Requests for permission to reproduce material from this
work should be sent to:

Permissions
Texas Review Press
English Department
Sam Houston State University
Huntsville, TX 77341-2146

Library of Congress Cataloging-in-Publication Data
Alcorn, Charles, 1961–
  Argument against the good-looking corpse / Charles
Alcorn. — 1st ed.
     p. cm.
  ISBN 978-1-933896-52-6 (pbk. : alk. paper) — ISBN
978-1-933896-53-3 (cloth : alk. paper)
  I. Title.
  PS3601.L3429A89 2010
  813'.6—dc22
                        2010039747

Cover and Book Design: David C. Felts
Cover Photo: Bruce Weber © 1984. Used by permission
of the photographer.

Acknowledgements

I wish to thank, first and foremost, my parents, Chuck and Dorothy Jean Alcorn, for their abiding love, steadfast support, and constant encouragement. This book is for you.

I would like to gratefully acknowledge *The Texas Review* Publisher Paul Ruffin and Fiction Editor Eric Miles Williamson for publishing this collection and for their skillful editing, sage advice, and uncanny ability to actualize dreams.

Finally, I'd like to bear-hug Charles and William for being the finest boys imaginable and genuflect in the direction of Angela for being her wildly enthusiastic self, and *the* loveliest Muse.

Contents

Shall a man lose himself in countless adjustments, and be so shaped with reference to this, that and the other, that the simply good and healthy and brave parts of him are reduced and clipp'd away?

—Walt Whitman

Howdy from the Big House

Mission Valley, Texas
May 12, 2006

Since taking up residence in this elbow of Eden, this former pig farm/meth lab on the banks of Coleto Creek, I've been reading a lot of the Big Yawp. And it's pretty clear, upon closer inspection, that my life's been clipped.

But only temporarily. And only in the most benevolent way.

My father's life, on the other hand, has been clipped in the blindside, smashmouth *what-the-hell-just-hit-me?* way. Some kind of gut cancer. Real bad. Metastasized. Out of control. In a word—done, though my father would never admit to such a thing. And neither do I.

The doctors give him five months. Which, of course, I am absolutely convinced he'll stretch into a year. He is that willfully optimistic. That tough. Or maybe stoic is more like it. At any rate, the upshot is…

Chuck Wooten's getting his affairs in order, and so am I.

Which is why I'm under house arrest. Not of the legal variety, but of the handshake kind. An unregulated agreement between parents and their adult child. Oh, and the behavioral specialists at Walden Pond.

I am currently sequestered in a domicile off Farm to Market 447 in Victoria County, on thirty acres of rolling coastal plain. Down a caliche road between two unincorporated wide spots in the road called Nursery and Weesatche. I live in a house purchased with windfall profits from an Austin Chalk gusher, a seldom used second home, perfect for the work at hand.

By modern urban standards, my location is remote. But not in the west Texas sense. Living in Big Spring, Texas. For 22 months. In Howard County. That's remote. Though I was never lonely in Big Spring, as you will see.

I am watched over by a most trusted man— Hipolito Sustaita-Galvan. Miss Flannery once said that, "a good man is hard to find"—not in this part of the country. She would have cottoned to Hipolito Galvan.

The month is March. 2006 AD. The season is freshly scalding, blanket wet, mosquito sucking South Texas spring. Thankfully, the air conditioning works like arctic breath.

My mission is to explain to my father, in writing, what's become of me since I left my cradle of Gatsby-like pleasure for the salt-watered gridiron; the sand-blown oval at Permian A&I; since receiving undeserved redemption in South Oak Cliff, since recording ten consecutive personal bests in Barcelona (and still finishing out of the medals) then dreamily unraveling in a hundred other-worldly ports of call; since my impaling in Oslo, since facing the ghost of Mr. Elmo high above the Philippine Sea; since lounging like a happy otter in the brackish inlets of Aransas Pass; since my final touchdown in the sands of the Sonoran Desert; since swallowing whole the offerings of a savior maiden.

But it's not as if I haven't kept in touch. I return, faithfully, every year, to my blood's country. To my mother and father. For wing shooting in the winter and golf in the summer. And holidays too.

It's true that a young man can keep his prized perception in place, and ugly reality under wraps, if he maintains filial piety and doesn't borrow too much money. But my parents know what's apparent to the outside world. I need to dig deeper; reveal the soft underbelly.

Actually, it'll be good to reconstruct just what the hell I've been doing. Dad will be proud of the stuff he knows and a bit perplexed by the stuff he doesn't. But I doubt he'll be surprised.

As long as the limbs were lithe and supple, as long as contests were held between lines of chalk, the simplicity of my life was breathtaking. But such is the fleeting nature of sinew stretched taut, snapped and frayed.

Yes, since shedding my thinclads, for the robes of commerce, my returns have diminished. Meanwhile, Dad has carefully cashiered his days, months and years. Tracking scents borne on ancient coastal gusts—getting richer, wiser, and closer to thee My Lord.

Anyway, the house where I'm being kept under lock and key is spacious. I rest in a soft bed. I watch sports via satellite. I heat and eat meals prepared at the local HEB supermarket after which I repair to a wrap-around porch featuring a limestone fire pit of astounding dimension centered beneath the spreading branches of a fine old oak which provides shade for my rough-hewn rocking chair and roost to several varieties of bird including mocking, field larks, mourning and white wing dove, and on occasion, a solitary turkey buzzard, who lights on an uppermost limb and waits for whom I do not know.

Although I ask of her, all the time, "who you looking for?"

It is a comfortable house, but I am not comfortable in it.

My days are simple: Rise, exercise, write, eat, revise, eat, rock, watch, read, rest. I do not drink. I do not drug. I refuse to inject or swallow.

The one challenge I see with this lovely incarceration is the total absence of women—the undeniable constant through all these years. In fact, I would say, the insatiable, dogged pursuit of a woman's undivided attention has been the root cause of our (me and Dad's) lives. Not the root problem. Not the root celebration. No, the object of our desires, the motherwifelover, is our endgame.

Absolutely. It gets complicated. Our relations with women cannot be characterized as healthy, modern or neat. But we sure as hell aren't haters. So, perhaps a period of enforced celibacy; a period of what the Big Yawp refers to, as "disinterested reflection", will do me good; will provide needed perspective. Because, I suppose, there are reasons why I'm under watchful care. Although I always beg to differ.

No, in fact, I'm relieved to be under arrest. I'm pleased to be blocked from chasing the next opportunity. I'm glad to be moving down a fresh-cut *sendero*, cleared of brush and pear, shackled to the keyboard, typing my way out of the thicket. And all the while, a mere fifteen minutes drive from my childhood home.

In reading this anxious recounting of rock-solid myths and sirius cloud conjecture, this *tejano* mélange of hope and want, my father will be shocked to discover his son. Of that I have no doubt. As the pages turn in his warm, frail hands, my father, a man who I respect almost too deeply, will read of a son who circulates, for the most part, in the ethers; touches down when propriety dictates. And never for long. A prodigal in search of a place, a mate, a calling that leaves him quiet. A peace that allows him to simply close his eyes and sleep.

That's it. That's the plan. I'll keep you posted.

Argument Against the
Good-Looking Corpse

Weesatche, Texas
January 24, 1981

I feel weird doing this. But this guy, Marcus
Matula, told me to on this tape. He wants me to write
down what he said on the tape, and I guess it's the least
I can do, since he killed himself.

I'm a pretty good writer. I'm on the Jet Bulletin
staff and I'm secretary for the Key Club. But this is a
lot different than writing a story for the school paper.

I've already listened to the tape once. On the tape
recorder. It seems weird that he left a tape recorder in
the barn. I mean the whole thing's weird. But especially
the tape recorder, because it's a real old one—not like
a Walkman, but like an old junky one from JC Penney.

But Marcus did give me some good advice at the

very first. He said, "don't worry, just act like you're talking to me and write it all down." So that's what I'm doing—I mean that's what I'm going to do—I'm practicing right now. I like to write, except it takes a long time.

Marcus and me are going steady. And you know, this might be the first time I've ever seen him sit still since we've been dating. But that's weird. I guess we're not going steady any more. He's lying over there by the pen where he keeps his show steer. I don't think the steer knows what's going on yet.

But before I get started with his stuff I better explain my stuff. How this whole thing got started. I'm a senior, and a lot of people say I look like Cher, and I knew Marcus was attracted to me because he used to whistle real loud when he and his cowboy friends came to the basketball games. I was embarrassed at first because I was supposed to be concentrating on my cheers—I'm head cheerleader—but I thought he was pretty cute even though he was only a sophomore. But he looked older. He's got a real good body, like Mad Max, except he's a kicker.

Anyway, he may have looked mature, but he didn't act it. He did crazy things when he got drunk. Like the first time we broke up. He put bologna slices all over my car and it took the paint off in perfect little circles. That was the first time I ever heard my Dad cuss. That was wild.

And he always has that nasty dip in his mouth. I told him when we started dating that he couldn't dip when we went out and he had to act more mature if he was going to date a senior because I was taking a real chance dating a sophomore. But all my friends said he was real cute and it didn't matter if I dated a younger guy because all the cute seniors were already taken and the rest were dorks, and besides, I was head cheerleader and I could date anybody I wanted.

And Marcus did have a neat truck. He was real proud of it. He said the tires cost two hundred and fifty dollars apiece. It was jacked-up and you could see forever when we drove into town even though we couldn't order at the Sonic because it wouldn't fit under the roof. So we used to park across the street at the Captain's Table parking lot.

So anyway, we dated for about six weeks, and I guess he really liked me, because we did it a lot. A lot of girls are scared to admit it, but every girl in my class has done it, except maybe Belinda Ohrt—she's the assistant principal's daughter. And it's really dumb because everybody does it and runs and tells their best friend, but if anybody but their best friend asks them if they've done it, they won't say.

I don't mind saying.

But I had no idea how strongly Marcus felt about it. He told me on the tape that he kept count. You'd think only girls would do stuff like keep count. Fifty-seven times, I think that's what he said. Marcus wasn't my first, because I'm a senior, but I don't think he knew. I didn't want to hurt his feelings.

It was pretty nice when we used to come out here on the weekend, after the dances, and crawl up in the hayloft. Maybe it was because we were drunk. I shouldn't say that, but God he was goofy. One time he climbed down the ladder and ran around the pasture all naked. Then he started howling at the coyotes. Marcus was crazy. But I guess I shouldn't say that either, now.

Anyway, so he left me a note on my car this morning that said he was going to kill himself and that he hoped I felt bad—which I guess meant that I *should* feel bad about him catching me and Morgan Wooten at the drive-in. I thought Marcus was going to be at the Fat Stock show all night because he was showing his calf. So I told Morgan I'd meet him at the drive-in after the basketball game on Saturday night. But then Marcus caught us in the back seat of Morgan's Blazer. I told Morgan we should have turned the stereo down, but he just had to show off his new Pioneer speakers. Then maybe Marcus wouldn't have been able to sneak up on us like that. But no, he's got Boston cranked as loud as it can go.

And boy was Marcus ever mad. Pounding on the windows and cussing up a storm—wow, was he cussing. Morgan was trying to calm him down, but Marcus said he was going to go get his 12-gauge, and that's when Morgan said he better get the hell out of Dodge, and gave me a kiss, then ran over to Randal Thibodeaux's truck.

And would you believe that Marcus actually came back and blew the side mirror off Morgan's Blazer. Scared me to death. I mean, I knew he wouldn't shoot me, but still. I crawled out the very back, when Marcus was coming around the front, and ran over kind of sneaky, and made one of the JV cheerleaders drive me home.

I guess it was pretty bad. Somebody said that Marcus was so mad, when he found out that I left, that he walked up to that huge screen and shot Mel Gibson right in the mouth. Then he got back in his truck and tore out after Randal and Morgan. Probably chased them to Cuero for all I know. I never did see Morgan at school today.

I guess I should have realized right then that Marcus was taking things a little too seriously. But he was always doing stuff like that. He was so jealous. He said on the tape my shirt was off, but that's not true— we were only kissing. Besides, Morgan's kind of shy, or something. I mean, in all the time Morgan had in that back seat, Marcus would've had me all the way naked. But all Morgan got off was my shirt. He probably tried to get my bra off, but it's kind of hard. Even for me sometimes.

Anyway, I've got to stop thinking about that, and think about Marcus. I've got to stop for a minute. I'd kinda like to look at him, but I'm not. He hung himself with baling wire, and I guess after a while, the rafter broke. I bet it hurt. I can't believe he really did it.

Boy.

So anyway, I thought he was just kidding in the note. It was kind of weird, but I thought he was just kidding, so I went to school because I didn't want to miss cheerleading practice. We're working on this new pyramid thing that everybody thinks is real danger-ous, but it's easy, once you know how. So I really didn't remember about Marcus, until after practice. I told some people at lunch about how mad he was about catching me and Morgan at the drive-in, but they said he was just being queer. I thought he was just being queer, too.

So anyway, so I drove out to Marcus's house after practice—they live about fifteen miles from town—and there it was, Marcus's big ol' truck, parked under the little shed he built for it. And I knew everything was going to be okay because I like Marcus a lot more than Morgan.

I peeked inside the house first, but the only person I saw was Mr. Matula passed out at the kitchen table. I sure hope he's still asleep.

Anyway, so I tippy-toed around the house and came down here to the barn because I thought maybe Marcus was grooming his calf. Turns out Marcus's calf got Reserve Champion at the Fat Stock show. I think that calf was the only thing Marcus cared about besides me. He treated that thing like his baby—always washing and combing him all the time. He even blow dried the dang thing's hair.

Maybe that's why he did it. Maybe he thought he was mad about catching Morgan and me, but he was really sad about his calf going to the butcher.

Makes me sad.

I thought he was asleep when I first came in because he didn't move at all. He was kind of lying on his side where I couldn't see his face, and I started playing with him, kicked him kind of—not hard—but he still didn't move. So I got down and was going to surprise him—give him a kiss. And that's when I screamed. His tongue was hanging out a mile, and it was blue!

Then I started crying because I didn't really think that he would do it. But he did. And I couldn't believe he was serious, because I didn't think we were that serious. Then I didn't know what to think.

And then after a while I saw the tape recorder and that's when things started getting really weird because I thought maybe, maybe Marcus was the kind of guy who'd do something stupid, but not the kind of guy who would leave some message on a tape recorder.

I guess he had the whole thing planned out, and I started feeling dumb because I thought Marcus was just another dumb guy in the FFA. I guess all kickers aren't dumb, but there's only one I know of in the National Honor Society.

So I started looking at the tape recorder. It was the kind with two big spools, where you can see all the tape. It was sitting on a bale of hay next to him. I don't know why I didn't see it when I first came in. I guess I thought it was a piece of farm equipment or something. And it was plugged into one those long orange extension cords all the way to the electricity box and luckily I know how to run tape recorders because I used one last summer when I was a Pink Lady at Citizen's Hospital. We used it with kids who had speech problems.

Anyway, I listened to the tape, and it was weird, especially when he started talking about me—I want to listen to that part again. You're not going to believe what he said about me, if I can find it.

I can't find it.

I think it was somewhere in the beginning—but what he said was that he knew I was better looking than the Wrangler billboard lady—it's this big billboard on the way out to Marcus's house—and he wanted to drive me to wherever they took billboard pictures and make me the new Wrangler girl. Then he said after I got my picture on the billboard he wanted to get his Dad and show him he was dating the Wrangler girl.

I bet that's when he started thinking about hanging himself. I bet he got jealous again. God, he used to get so mad when boys said things to me at the dances. He couldn't stand for anybody to even look at me. It got to where he was getting in a fight every time we went. That's one of the reasons I went to the drive-in with Morgan.

Can you believe it? He probably started thinking about how everybody would be looking at my butt on that billboard and it just drove him all-the-way crazy. I can just see him. His face used to get real red when he was mad. Isn't that crazy?

Then he said some stuff about his mother after the billboard stuff—she got killed in a car wreck when he was little—but you could tell he was still thinking about the billboard. Then he said he hated his Dad. He didn't say why. He probably hated him because he had to do chores all the time. Marcus always told me he hated doing chores.

Then he said some pretty mean things about me, too. I guess I shouldn't blame him—you could tell he was getting crazy—but I couldn't believe he called me a whore. That made me feel pretty bad. I went out to the car and was going to leave but then I started feeling guilty. I got my spiral notebook and came back down and here I am.

I just read this over and I don't think it's what Marcus had in mind. But I really don't have time to write down all the stuff Marcus wanted me to right now because my parents are probably wondering where I am, and Mr. Matula's probably going to wake up any minute now, and it's getting kind of spooky out here. Plus, I can't miss the game tonight because I'm on top of the pyramid.

Bye Marcus.

Pipe Dreams

Victoria, Texas
June 2, 1983

His bad dream was over, but the normal starchy
freshness of Morgan Wooten's childhood room was
gone, replaced by the sheet-staining funk of night
sweats. A single rivulet trickled down his back. He
wrestled his legs free from the sheets, sat up on the
side of the bed, and stared, blank-faced, at the clock
radio. The sterile blue-green numbers 3:45 cast a sickly
glow on his smooth skin, already deeply tanned after
a week of roughnecking in the blistering South Texas
oil fields.

"Hell with this, man," Morgan cursed, but not
loud enough to wake his parents sleeping down the
hall. "Who the hell says I have to roughneck?"

He collapsed back into the dank heap of sheets

and pillows, stomach-churning nervous about having to return to the scene of his "accident." In less than four hours he'd be back out there trying to live down "dropping the pipe." Trying not to be the greenass boss's son. Trying to prove himself, again.

He punched a pillow into shape; mumbled something about going back to goddamn sleep. Rite of passage my ass, he thought, recalling, from the week before, his father's expected invitation to roughneck for Wooten Well Service. "It'll be good for you."

Morgan agreed.

Until he dropped seventy-two joints of pipe down a 10,000-foot hole.

"I'm a fucking ballplayer," he seethed, watching an Earl Campbell bobblehead, in Oiler Columbia Blue, nod in agreement from his perch on Morgan's bedroom desk. "I'm not some dog-ass roughneck. Got no damn business being out there."

Dawn was still twenty minutes away, but already, there were a herd of trucks gathered around Junior's general store and truck stop near the crest of Goldman's Hill. Among the oilfield pickups, electricians van's and painter's panel trucks was Morgan's spectacular '79 Blazer—a perfectly accessorized 4-wheel drive behemoth, complete with 8-inch lift kit, Monster Mudder tires, and an ear-splitting stereo.

As soon as Morgan ejected his prized bootleg Asleep at the Wheel cassette, and stepped out into the morning's humid cool, he recognized the outrageous bulk of Darryl Matusak's '69 Impala turning in off the

Goliad Highway at reckless speed. The dust-covered four-door rolled into the acre-wide gravel parking lot and skidded to a stop next to a row of ice boxes aligned down Junior's west side. Morgan could feel his stomach cramping as he walked up to his driller to see if he could help with the water bucket, or anything at all.

"Mornin' Darryl," he said, still unsure, this time of day, whether he should be raring to go, or quiet.

Morgan reached to shake his hand, but Darryl threw Morgan his key chain instead. "Fill up the Igloo. To the *top* this time," the driller said, looking all serious at his employer's son, as if he were talking to some pre-schooler. As he if he had no idea Morgan was an All-State linebacker with a full ride at Permian A&I; not some greenass boss's son.

"And be sure to nudge them two cinder blocks up against it," Darryl added with a smart-ass smile. "So it won't tump over this time."

Morgan wanted to tell him that if he'd slow the fuck down, the cooler was plenty heavy enough to stay put without the cinder blocks.

"Will do," he said, to Darryl's back, as the driller walked his sausage legs briskly inside.

Born and bred south Texas Czech, Darryl Matusak was what Sister Ernestine, Morgan's AP English teacher, would have referred to as a "meticulous" person.

"A perfectionist" she might have added.

"Pain in the ass" is what Morgan called him, though he had to admit the young driller did have undeniable skills. The way the twenty-eight year old handled the rig's brake and throttle, how he made the double Cat engines sing, was impressive.

"I'll make tool pusher before I'm thirty," he'd assured Morgan, when they'd met the week before. "Or go work for Patterson the next day. You can tell your Daddy I said so."

Morgan was going to get right on that, but just now, he was stuck in the water line, with the rest of the greenasses, rehearsing his Darryl comebacks. Thankfully, comic relief was just seconds away, as the derrickman, Ricky Delgado, stumbled out of the passenger seat of a purple Ford Falcon. The driver, a wild-eyed woman with heavy blue eye shadow and a tremendous slash of cleavage, looked perfectly sexy to Morgan; even more so when she nailed Ricky in the shoulder with a heavy foil packet. In spite of this public insult, and in the face of a spew of Spanish profanities, Ricky leaned in the window to give the woman a kiss.

She blocked his mouth with her hand.

"Why you want to be like that?" he asked, reaching down to pick up the packet of soft tacos off the gravel.

She yelled a little more, shot her common-law husband the finger, then peeled out, peppering Ricky with a rooster tail of gravel.

Morgan tried to keep his eyes on his Red Wings when Ricky walked by, but ended up saying good morning anyway.

"What's fucking good about it, man?" Ricky asked.

Oh, Jesus, Morgan thought, but Rick's smile put him at ease.

"Just kidding, man. What's up, *pendejo?*"

"*Nada mucho*, Rick," said Morgan. "*Que pasa?*"

"Pretty good Spanish for a white boy," Ricky said, punching Morgan on the shoulder.

"Really? You think so?"

"Hell no," he said, laughing. "You sound like my *pendejo* priest at Sorrows."

Ricky Delgado, and his lethargic sense of humor, was the perfect antidote to Darryl's dour work ethic. Since migrating from the town of San Luis Potosi at twelve, Ricky'd fathered four kids by two wives, been shot once (gut shot, great scar) and thrown in jail more times than he wanted to admit. He had the emotional stability of a lit firecracker, but of the crew, Ricky was Morgan's favorite—the kind of man who kept things in perspective—not just hauling ass and busting ass every minute like jarhead Darryl.

Morgan was lugging the water cooler back to the Impala, when the fourth member of the crew, Mike McNeely, a rising sophomore at Texas A&M with the typical Irish red mop and freckles, barely got out of the passenger seat before his dad pulled back on to the Goliad highway. Morgan had overheard that McNeely's dad lost his shrimp boat and had had to go to work for one of the competing Vietnamese outfits in Seadrift.

No damn good was all Morgan knew about what was going on between the KKK and the Lavaca Bay refugees. And he sure as hell wasn't going to make small talk with Mike about it.

"How's it hanging?" asked Morgan.

"TGIF, baby," said Mike, as Morgan slammed the Impala's trunk shut and they all piled in. "Ain't nothing but good, on payday."

"That's right," Morgan said, sliding across the slick vinyl front seat. "My first roughnecking paycheck."

"And you best cash your check with Mr. Junior," Darryl said, settling in behind the wheel. "He only takes a dollar fifty out, and the grocery store charges you two."

"Sounds good," Morgan said, wondering why the driller was staring at him. "Anything else I need to know about the world of oilfield banking?"

"Naw, I don't imagine you got any worries about money," said Darryl, drumming his fingers on the steering wheel. "But you are in Ricky's seat."

"Ah, damn," said Morgan, whipping around in time to catch the derrickman giving him the stink eye. "Sorry, Rick."

"How many times do I have tell your greenass?" said Darryl, turning the ignition and revving the engine. "Driller drives, derrickman's shotgun…"

"I know, I know," said Morgan, crawling over the top of the seat, just so he could stick his ass in Darryl's face. "Floorhands in the back."

Morgan high-fived Mike, who rolled his eyes, then fell into an instant, snoring sleep.

As Morgan watched the rising sun turn the dew-covered prairie into a blanket of wet pearls, he pondered the absurdity of his situation. He knew exactly why he was roughnecking: his buddy Dennis worked at his dad's Ford dealership; his buddy Randal hauled hay for his dad; his buddy Gerard pumped gas at his dad's Texaco station. That's what guys around Victoria did when they outgrew Little League; they worked for their dads. The only problem for Morgan was that in spite of following his dad around workover rigs all his life, he was no "born roughneck." In fact, Morgan had no mechanical smarts whatsoever. He couldn't even remember "righty tighty, lefty loosey" half the time.

As Darryl punched the Impala's V-8, and they flew across the Coleto Creek bridge at a smooth eighty miles per hour, Morgan thought it was looking like a damn long summer; lucrative, but damn long. Boss's son, two left thumbs and fourteen-hour work days. He had no idea how he was going to make it through eleven more weeks of this crap. All he did know was what he lacked in know-how, he'd have make up with giddy-up.

I can handle this stuff, he thought, as Darryl pulled off the Refugio highway into the sprawling O'Connor Field and started his bat out-of-hell routine over the washboard ranch road to the well site. A&I doesn't give full rides to just anyone; even if it is D-II. At least I'll be in shape for two-a-days.

"Hey, wake up sleepy heads. We're almost there," Darryl said, as the Impala rolled to a stop beside the "doghouse," a portable metal hut where the rough-necks changed clothes and ate lunch.

"Another day, another dollar," mumbled McNeely, as he sat facing Morgan and Ricky, practically knee-to-knee, pulling on knee-high rubber boots with steel toes and sweat-stained clothes.

"Yes sir, got to go to work," said Ricky, in his funny border monotone." Gotta make a dollar so we can suck some Lone Star *cerveza* tonight."

"You drink that crap?" questioned McNeely. "A real man's gotta drink Shiner, ain't it, Morgan?"

"Shiner. Lone Star," Morgan said, delighted to finally be included in the doghouse conversation. "As long as it's brewed in Texas."

"Hell, y'all are full of it," said Darryl, stuffing the crusty legs of his Wranglers into his boots. "A real man's got to drink Bud."

"All you gringos want to do is argue, man," said Ricky, stripping down to a pair of grungy briefs. "I just drink to slow down. Who gives a fuck what kind of beer it is?"

"Better throw them clothes on," said Darryl, sneaking a peek outside. "Harpy's already walking around."

"Fuck Harpy," said Ricky, zipping up a pair of red coveralls over his skivvies. "He needs to quit drinking all that goddamn coffee, man. Motherfucker makes me nervous."

"Just get your asses out here, will you?" said Darryl, stomping toward the rig. "We're burning daylight."

Once the driller was out of earshot, Morgan asked, "Hey, Rick, how come he's always in such a bad mood?"

"Hell, how come you're always in such a *good* mood?" Ricky said. "Me and Darryl, we ain't like you college boys. This is it for us. Know what I mean?"

"Yeah, I hear you," Morgan said. "Need to just shut up and work."

"There you go, brother," Ricky said, rapping his knuckles on Morgan's hardhat on his way out of the doghouse. He cleared the door, but then came back, leaned in as Morgan searched under the benches for his gloves. "I don't mean to be fucking with you, man, but you know, it's different for us full-time people. This ain't summer; this is every day. Darryl's okay, he just gets in a hurry is all."

"That's cool, seriously. I know what you mean," Morgan said, talking from his hands and knees. "Hey, you wouldn't happen to have an extra pair of gloves would you?"

Looking up, he wished he hadn't asked.

"Hell no," Ricky said, turning toward the rig. "What the fuck you coming out here with no gloves? Ask Mike, he might have some."

Which was the last thing Morgan wanted to do as he walked toward the circle of four standing next to the rig, listening to the idling diesel engines.

"Morning, Mr. Harpy," Morgan said, willing himself to act cool in spite of feeling like a complete loser with no gloves. "What's in store for this beautiful Friday."

"You're going to love it," said Darryl. "Picking us up a big ass string today, boy."

Morgan asked, "And what exactly is a big ass string?"

"You'll find out in about five minutes," interrupted Mr. Harpy, a ramrod straight, crew cut, permanently sunburned veteran of the south Texas oilfields and one of Wooten Well Service's best toolpushers. "See that cloud of dust kicking up over yonder?"

They all turned to look in the direction of the Refugio highway.

"That's two trucks worth of two and seven-eight's inch tubing. Run about 30 feet a joint. Two hundred pounds apiece."

"Sounds heavy," Morgan said, looking at McNeely for confirmation.

"No shit," McNeely said, picking at a scab on his elbow. "Man, are we ever going to earn that check today."

"That's right boys; time to pick up," said Darryl. "And the faster you unload and tally that pipe, the faster we can get it in the hole."

"Doesn't sound too bad," Morgan said, breaking from the circle of men to look under the rig for stray gloves. "I helped unload about five hundred bales of alfalfa last summer; those fuckers weighed at least a hundred."

"So, this your first time to pick up, Morgan?" asked Mr. Harpy.

"Yes, sir," Morgan said. "Just about everything's my first time."

"I heard that," Darryl agreed.

"Well, you picked a dandy to learn on," said Mr. Harpy, taking off a Schlumberger gimme hat to smooth his thick blonde bristles. "Company man called me up last night and said that Quintana decided to make a saltwater disposal well out of this one."

"You know what that means, Morgan?" Darryl taunted, as he unhooked the cat line from the side of the derrick.

"No."

"Means it's some heavy fucking pipe, and you got 365 joints to throw them elevators around," he said, laughing. "You're going to *wish* you were hauling hay after a couple of hours of this shit."

"At least he don't have to bust his nuts dragging'

those heavy mothers up to the floor," added Ricky, grabbing his crotch in mock agony.

"What the hell, Mike?" implored Morgan, after Mr. Harpy left them to meet the circling gin pole trucks. "Picking up sucks, huh?"

"Long fucking day," Mike said, taking the cat line from Darryl and throwing a loop around the Christmas Tree—a two-ton contraption that kept wells from blowing out. "That's all I can tell you."

"Help him out, Morgan!" Darryl yelled, when the Christmas Tree started getting away from Mike. "How come I got to tell you every little fucking thing to do?"

"How 'bout 'cause it's my fifth day on the job," Morgan muttered, grabbing on to the cat line, helping Mike push the tree off to the side of the wellbore.

"Say what?" Darryl snapped.

"Nothing, man," Morgan said. "Say, where's the toilet paper?" He could feel the adrenaline wreaking havoc on his bowels. "I got to take care of some business."

"In the rig cab, behind the seat," yelled Mr. Harpy, as the roustabouts rolled out of the trucks. "Watch out for them fire ants. They're all over, since that last rain."

"Thanks, Mr. Harpy."

Man, wouldn't you know it, Morgan thought, as he trudged out on to the bald prairie to relieve his straining colon. Just when I'm fixin' to make it through this week, we go and pick up a load of the heaviest pipe in South Texas. Fucking A!

He was squatting behind a huisache sapling when he spotted an enormous black fire ant mound, practically covering the base of a live oak.

Hell with those fire ants. I'll give them something to chew on, he thought, high-stepping over clumps of buffel grass, pants around his ankles, to the black conical pile. He positioned himself precisely and proceeded to drown the ants under a torrent of diarrhea. He stood for a minute amazed by the disgusting, mocha-fudge frenzy.

"Look at those little bastards!" he said, finally leaping away when several dozen started crawling up his boots.

"*Bon appetit*, fellas."

Walking back, Morgan saw the roustabouts from the pipe truck were already unchaining the tubing from the frame of the gin pole trucks. He immediately tore out for the doghouse. "I've GOT to find a pair of gloves," he said. He frantically pushed over the doghouse trash barrel and began sifting through the detritus in hopes of salvaging a discarded pair of gloves. He finally found two. Both left-handed.

"Come on, Morgan. Haul your ass, will you," yelled Darryl. "Help those wets start unloading that shit."

"I'm coming. Hold your horses, man." Morgan yelled, over the roar of the diesels, trying to pull on the odd-handed glove.

Morgan and McNeely had the chore of lifting each joint off the flatbed trailer and heaving it on to the pipe rack. It took over an hour of constant motion to unload, stack and tally the pipe.

"Better grab some water, boys," said Mr. Harpy. "Y'all are sweating worse than a high noon whore."As they gathered around the water cooler Darryl started his daily tirade on the stupidity of the white-collar world.

"Mr. Harpy says that pipe's brand new," Darryl said, jerking his thumb at the four-deep rack of tubing.

"Seems strange to use new pipe on a saltwater disposal well," said Morgan.

"Hell, them bean counters in town, they don't know their ass from a hole in the ground," Darryl said. "All they do is sign them division orders. Who cares what it costs."

"Wouldn't make a damn if that pipe was made of gold," Ricky said, wrapping ice cubes inside a bright red bandana. "I'm still going to bust my ass."

"Get your wet friends to help you out," suggested McNeely, pointing to the roustabouts sitting on the pipe rack.

"They ain't my friends, *pendejo*."

"Bet you'll let'em help you out."

"Hell, yeah, what you think?" Ricky asked, tying the bulging bandana behind his head. "I'm going to drag that shit up the floor by myself? That's for dumb gringos like you, McSqueely."

"Ah, shut up, Rick," said McNeely, "Can't you tell I was kidding?"

"Naw, McSqueely," Ricky said, draining the water from his paper cup. "Sometimes I don't know what the fuck you're talking about."

"Sure hope those elevators are working right," Morgan said.

This was met with the crumpling of paper cups, and Darryl's audible sigh. "Let's go," said the driller. "Let's get this sorry ass pipe in the hole."

The sun glowed on the horizon as they trudged silently back to the rig floor. Lunch was still two hours away, plenty of time to work up a sweat.

Darryl leapt up to the driller's stand and cranked the rig engines. The twin Cat diesels coughed, then broke into steady song. Mr. Harpy walked over to his Wooten Well Service pickup, raised the hood so his engine wouldn't overheat, then watched intently from the air-conditioned cab as the crew, in a flurry of activity, prepped for the intricate monotony of going down the hole.

Ricky made up a six-foot sub and packer on the pipe rack while Morgan and Mike were attaching the elevators to the block. After Darryl secured the packer in the hole, Ricky and another roustabout picked a joint off the rack and dragged it to the floor. McNeely took the joint from Ricky, and with a mighty heave, threw the pipe up into the jaws of the elevators which Morgan slammed shut after which Darryl whisked the joint off the rack and up the derrick until its full length hung above the hole.

In rapid sequence, Morgan wire-brushed the pipe's bottom threads, slapped on a glob of dope, stabbed the joint into the top collar of the sub, and held backups as McNeely made up the connection with the hydraulic tongs. After the two joints were tight, Darryl raised up slightly on the block, allowing Morgan to disengage the "slips" holding the pipe in place above the open hole. Darryl lowered the joint down the hole until the top collar was waist high with Morgan, who then kicked the slips back around the pipe, unlatched the elevators, and pushed them away from the hole—ready for McNeely to lift the next joint Ricky had walked up from the pipe rack.

A seasoned crew could complete these single "trips" in a minute, or so. But Morgan's inexperience increased the time per trip considerably.

"Hell, boy," Darryl said, after about ten trips. "Can't you work them elevators any faster than that?"

"I'm trying. I think they need some grease or something," grunted Morgan, trying to close the hundred-pound jaws around a joint.

Darryl vaulted from the driller's stand to the floor, forcing Morgan to make way. He manhandled the elevators and slammed them shut around the pipe.

"Get rough with'em, boy," he said, beaming. "They ain't going to bite."

"No problem, coach."

"Hey, Daddy's boy," Darryl said, taking the brake handle off the chain. "You and me can go 'round and round. You hear me?"

"Is that right?," Morgan mumbled, unable to meet his glare.

"Fucking A, boy," Darryl said, sending the joint of pipe screaming down the hole. "Don't make me no difference what you're last name is."

"Hey, man, don't worry about Darryl," reassured McNeely, making up the next pipe connection. "He just gets in a hurry is all."

Morgan unlatched the elevators and waited for the next joint. This go-around his timing was perfect. A broad smile spread below Morgan's hardhat after slamming the elevators around a new joint. "Piece a cake, man," he said, as he kicked the slips and another joint slid deep into the earth. "Easy Bake Cake."

Even Daryl smiled at that one.

The crew soon found a steady rhythm and the stack of tubing began to disappear rapidly. Ricky bantered with the roustabouts in Spanish while Morgan and McNeely talked mindlessly about Southwest Conference football. They had almost half of the pipe in the hole when Morgan noticed Jake Holloway's red company pickup making its way toward the rig.

"Here comes the company man," Morgan said.

Mr. Harpy turned off the Ag Report on the radio in time to hustle out to meet Mr. Jake. They shook hands, watched the crew put three more joints in the hole, then shouted at Darryl to shut her down.

"Don't have to ask me twice," Darryl said, hitting the kill switch then jumping off the driller's stand.

"Gee, that was some super-duper fun, ain't it?" said Morgan, kicking the slips around the last joint.

"Yeah, I can't wait to pick up the rest of those suckers in the heat of the day," sighed McNeely, stretching his red, swollen arms.

Jake Holloway, Quintana's Refugio-area supervisor, approached the rig. Jake probably wasn't much over sixty, but looked ancient. His face was windtooled purple and he walked with a pronounced limp, the result of a mishap in his roughnecking days. He'd been sitting on wells since the 40s and knew every hole—wet, dry or salty—in a six-county radius; called them his "children."

"Well, Mr. Jake," said Mr. Harpy, "where we going to eat dinner at?"

"Let's go over to Woodsboro," he said. "There's

a Mexican restaurant over there I want to try again."

"Why's that?" asked Mr. Harpy. "I thought them chili peppers didn't agree with you."

"Ah, I could give a hoot 'bout the food," Jake said, snorting. "It's the *senorita* servin' it I'm interested in." Jake revealed a few missing teeth when he smiled.

"Hell, Jake, you wouldn't know what to do with that stuff," said Darryl, pumping his groin double-time.

"Hell you say!" said Jake, punching the driller's shoulder. "There's still a lot of kick left in this mule."

"Well, y'all take your time; everything's under control," Darryl said. "Been throwing that iron down the hole like they was pixy sticks."

"Just make damn sure they're all strung together," said Mr. Harpy. He knew Darryl tended to get in hurry, especially on Friday afternoon.

"Never lost a joint in ten years," the driller said. "And we aim to keep it that way. Right, Morgan?"

"Oh you bet," Morgan mumbled, lowering himself down the floor ladder, trying to snap out of his "pipe tripping" fog.

As Jake and Mr. Harpy sped away through the midday mirages in route to their Tex-Mex feast, the roughnecks hunkered down with sack lunches and soda pop. Everyone sweated profusely in the doghouse's stifling heat.

"This thing tastes like papier-mâché," complained Morgan, about his soggy sandwich.

"What's paper mu-shay?" asked McNeely.

"It's French for ham and cheese on Mrs. Baird's."

"Oh."

Morgan pondered the term "doghouse" between

disgusted nibbles at his sandwich. Ricky guzzled his Thermos of Kool-Aid and picked at the soft tacos his wife had thrown at him. McNeely and Darryl were heartier eaters. They shared thick links of deer sausage and homemade pigs-in-a-blanket.

"Hey, Morgan, what you and Miss Victoria doing tonight?" asked McNeely.

"*No se*," said Morgan, not minding a bit that Darryl got to hear about his current good luck in the girlfriend department. "Probably go dancing. I think the Taylor Brothers are playing out at Weesatche Hall," he continued, daydreaming about his beauty queen/ track star's new skin-tight Calvin Klein's.

"Really? I wish I could go," said McNeely. "I'm working cattle out on Matagorda Island this weekend."

"Matagorda Island? Who the hell runs cows out there?," said Morgan, tossing the sandwich and setting in on an orange.

"Some rich ol' dude from Houston," Mike answered.

"I'd lose my gear if I had to do anything but sleep and eat this weekend."

"Yeah, boys, I tell you what I'm goin' to do," said Ricky, yawning. "I'm gonna fuck the dog. Pick up a case a beer and just fuck that dog, all weekend long."

"What the hell, Rick," said Morgan, smiling at the funny way the derrick men talked. "What the hell's that mean?" When Morgan looked up from the floor, Ricky was flipping him the bird and apparently really enjoying it.

"Well, boys, I hate to break up y'all's weekend planning, but we better hit it," said Darryl, closing up his lunch pail. "That pipe ain't going to jump in the hole by itself."

"Back to work!" barked Ricky, tossing a half-eaten taco into the trash barrel. *"¡Trabajo! ¡Trabajo!"*

Morgan knew he was going to need something besides a gallon of Delaware Punch in his system to make it through the afternoon heat. He fished a Snickers out of the bottom of his lunch sack and finished it in three bites.

"It's 105 degrees in Refugio," warned the KNAL DJ on the doghouse radio. "Better stay in the shade down that way."

"Yeah sure, buddy," griped Morgan, as he walked out into the glare, the dull roar of the diesels calling him to the rig.

Ricky woke up the roustabouts taking siesta under the pipe rack, while McNeely warmed up the tongs. Darryl gunned the motor impatiently as Morgan climbed the ladder to the rig floor.

"Come on man, you're always dragging ass," he yelled, bringing the block down from the derrick crown with terrifying speed.

The sharp squeal of the brakes startled Morgan so badly he almost fell off the ladder. "Hold your horses, Darryl. Fuck, man." Morgan still could not look him in the eye.

"Sure as hell couldn't go any slower."

Morgan grabbed the elevators and threw them around a joint.

Fucking dick, he thought. I gotta talk to McNeely and Rick, see what the fuck's up with this guy. What's he getting divorced, or something?

After McNeely made up a connection, Morgan kicked the slips and waited for the top collar. Again, Darryl brought the block down free fall. The whole rig shook as he stopped the collar inches from crushing the slips.

"Damn it, Morgan! Would you watch what you're doing'?" screamed Darryl, his face red with anger.

"What'd I do?"

Darryl pointed to the smoking slips.

"Oh, shit," Morgan grunted. "I...the vibration must have kicked them in."

"Not if you're paying attention to what you're fucking doing," yelled Darryl, jumping to the floor so he could get in Morgan's face. "You got the easiest fucking job out here and you're still screwing up. What the hell, boy? Let's go!"

McNeely watched as Darryl wheeled around and leapt back to the stand. Morgan stood glassy-eyed, with a white-knuckle grip on the elevators.

"Hey, take it easy, man," McNeely said. "Don't let him get to you."

"Fuck it!" screamed Morgan, exploding down on the slip pedal with his steel-toed boot.

For hours Morgan was speechless, concentrating on every repetitive detail, his entire body soaked with sweat and dope. Every so often he peered at the sun attempting to gauge the time, but was unsure. Finally, he snuck a peek at Darryl's pocket watch hanging by the cat line.

"Four o'clock, baby," he said. "One more hour, man, and we're out of here."

"Hey, all right. You can still talk," kidded McNeely,

watching the top collar of a joint screech to a halt. "You had me worried there for a while."

"Hell, man, don't worry about me. This boy can hang," laughed Morgan, as he kicked the slips and ripped open the elevators.

"NO-O-O-O!"

But Darryl's scream was too late.

The chain reaction was underway. Two hundred sixty-five joints of runaway pipe disappeared down the hole.

"No way! Please, God, No!"

Morgan dropped to his knees, staring into the hole.

"*Ay, chihuahua*," whistled Ricky, running up the pipe rack to take a look. "That's some fucked up shit, man."

"Damn, Morgan. Look at your hand!" said McNeely, pointing at his floor mate's bare left hand.

"I swear I kicked those slips in. I swear," coughed Morgan, oblivious to the blood seeping from a gash in his palm.

A thunderous crash signaled the end of the pipe's 10,000-foot fall. The sound of pipe crashing through forty feet of concrete plug caused Mr. Harpy to pour half a Thermos of coffee down his shirtfront.

"What the goddamn!" yelled Mr. Harpy, jumping out of the pickup, slapping rivulets of coffee off his shirt and pants.

Morgan sat back on his haunches. His first impulse was to jump off the floor and run, but he was frozen. Finally, he stood up. Blood rushed to his head. When his eyes cleared, Darryl's face was an inch away.

"Hey, fuckhead," Darryl spat, pointing at the empty maw of the slips. "Fucking sorry ass...Get the fuck off this rig."

"That's enough, Darryl," said Mr. Harpy, climbing on to the steel mesh floor and peering down into the hole. He stood, and whistled through his teeth; took off his cap to smooth his crew cut.

"All right, we got to fish that pipe out of the hole right now," he said. "Rick, get yourself a drink. Darryl, you and Mike take five, then get us a current tally, see what we got in the hole."

"Yes sir, Mr. Harpy," said Darryl and McNeely, almost simultaneously. The two jumped off the floor on to the pipe rack without giving Morgan another glance. Ricky walked over to Morgan who was leaning against the safety rail staring at his bleeding hand.

"Take it easy, man. This shit happens, *vato*," Ricky said, softly, patting Morgan's back. "I seen Darryl fuck up plenty a times. He knows it."

"Go on, Rick, get you some water," said Mr. Harpy, looking up from the hole, exchanging knowing smiles with his derrickman. Ricky could only shake his head as he climb down the greasy ladder to the ground.

Morgan took his hands off the railing and turned to face his toolpusher.

"You all right, son?"

"I'm all right," he said, flexing his hand, wiping the blood off what looked to be a small cut. "I'm really sorry, Mr. Harpy. I know better than that. Too big a hurry, I guess."

"Well, I ain't surprised," said Mr. Harpy. "Darryl knows better than to rush like that with a new hand.

But you got to pay attention, son."

"I've done it before, Mr. Harpy."

"Done what?" Mr. Harpy asked, looking none too pleased.

"Worked a whole summer for free," Morgan said, finally feeling the pressure inside his head drain a little. "I totaled my best friend's Mom's car on Memorial Day weekend and every penny I earned that summer, went straight to Atzenhoffer Chevrolet."

"Well, roughnecks don't pay for dropping pipe in the hole," said Mr. Harpy, shaking out an unfiltered Camel and putting it to his lips. "Wooten Well Service picks up the tab for this kind of thing. Ain't no different for you. You just got to be careful is all. Watch them elevators and slips every trip."

"Yes, sir, Mr. Harpy. I'll do it," Morgan said, "But Darryl kind of gets in a…"

Mr. Harpy cut him off with one raised eyebrow. "Just do your job, son. That's what your daddy hired you for."

Morgan hung his head, then squinted up at the toolpusher. "Absolutely, Mr. Harpy. I'll do it."

"Rise and shine folks. It's five 'til five on your work-a-day Monday," chirped the morning deejay on Morgan bedside radio.

Morgan threw his pillow at the offending machine. "Why? Why, do I have to go back out there?" His stomach was churning. The stitches in his left palm throbbed. A minute passed with no relief. Suddenly, he wrenched himself off the bed and pulled on a pair of jeans from a cardboard box labeled "work pants."

He padded around the room remembering how his dad hadn't cussed him when he got home; how they tallied at the kitchen table the cost of thirteen joints of 2 7/8" production tubing they needed to replace; how his dad had told him about an old Cajun driller in Thibodeaux, Louisiana who rode his ass when he accidentally kicked a pipe wrench down the hole.

Morgan tucked in the tattered shirttail of his father's khaki hand-me-down, then reached to turn out his bedroom light. Something fell out of his back pocket. He picked up the torn, left-handed glove, examined it briefly, then tossed it into the wastebasket.

Muscle-Bound Mojo
with a Colt .45

Big Spring, Texas
September 16, 1986

The sound of a man who's lost. Out here in the desert, somewhere. Lost it. Not his faculties. Not his sense of humor. But his short-term ability to communicate. To be understood.

What's that look like? Or, more to the point, what's that *sound* like?

You probably have an idea. You probably have some experience with crazy people (I'm being bad, we're not supposed to use the C word); some relative, some loved one, who's out of touch. Someone you can't quite reach, but hope to, as soon as possible. Someone whose dial won't tune. As if the words are familiar, but they just don't get it. You look them in

the face; you look them in the eye. You want to understand; want to be understood, but the connection is
broken. Gone.

I know it's frustrating. And kind of sad. Maybe
too sad to try.

But I wish you would.

We can all comprehend things beyond our reach.
Sometimes. If you try.

Anyway, I hope you'll give it a shot. Won't take
long.

They say I lost it the day I drove my truck into the
Odessa Meteor Crater. Could've been sooner. I might
have lost it the day I got gun-butted by my Marine drill
instructor during basic.

I can't really give you the precise coordinates of
my ungluing, but I will claim this much: Everybody
always said I was a model West Texas boy (an early-
70s model). Played football for the Mighty Mojos of
Odessa Permian, fought 411 days in Nam, came back
semi-whole, and graduated from Texas Tech with a BS
in Electrical Engineering. I married a San Angelo sheep
mogul's daughter, which was sweet, from the mohair
angle. Lots of sweaters in that deal. Lots of cashmere.
Plus, my wife modeled quite a variety of neck styles—
V, cowl, turtle—each quite fetching.

Anyway, we (me and my beautiful, Angora-
wearing wife) moved into a two-bedroom ranch-style
over by the University of Texas of the Permian Basin.
I was making forty grand a year as the microwave man
for ClayDesta Communications. Moving my family

right on into the 21st century.

Then up came the de-rail.

I was called out to minister to a microwave tower in Pyote. West of town, off Interstate 10. Some cables had blown haywire in a dust storm.

And man, I'm telling you, did I *not* see that crater coming.

Drove straight in. No brakes. No windshield wipers. No problem. Just like the rider in the ClayDesta ads whipping his horse across the South Plains—I nosedived that truck so deep into that crater they say my front bumper was up against my knees.

My legs were the problem, initially. Then my head. The head came later.

After several months of strenuous general hospital rehab, they put me in the Big Spring State Hospital, still gimpy from the waist down. I was nothing but wheelchair-bound brain bouncing off the walls. A skull kind of levitating above a body that looked presentable in Levi's and a crisp white button-down, but was otherwise pretty skinny.

The first year, I lost touch with my wife, though I still had a big crush on her sweater sets. I was a little preoccupied with the Wizard of Oz. All that energy. Did you know that tornados produce as much kinetic energy as an atomic warhead?

The second year, my parents pretty much packed it back to Victoria. Bless their hearts. Mom especially. I told her it was okay. She couldn't stay with me forever.

After that, I talked to myself a lot, because none of my buddies on the ward seemed to have the energy. I didn't complain. I had a bed by the window. Most of the guys, all they had to look at were cinder blocks. Not that much was going on outside. Nothing but horny toads bopping, and rocks sliding down the side of Scenic Mountain. Maybe the stray condom caught in the talus.

The third year, my legs weren't any better; they weren't any worse. Just heavy. And pretty numb.

I didn't pay Zamarillo much mind, at first. But I did make note of the *culebra* winding around her breast pocket, stitched in red thread. Then I remembered my father's own nursery school angel; stories of a woman who haunted his tubercular dreams in the far away sanatorium of San Angelo.

After a few more sessions, I noticed she had wonderful rhythm, like the Amp meter waves. Like my friend Hipolito when he shadow-boxed between the beds. She squirted Tiger Balm into her palm and rubbed my thighs in a circular motion, then up and down across my calves.

I asked Hipolito to translate for me, but he was too shy.

"How 'bout a new leather jump rope?"

"Okay, crazy *vato*," Hipolito sang, "What you want me to say?"

He explained to Zamarillo how deeply I appreciated her rubbing and how beautiful I thought she was. They blushed at each other across my thighs, and I blushed too. The blood felt wonderful in my legs.

She never said a word. Just hummed her magical sounds, as the orderlies bobbed and shuffled, pushing wet mops. Their footwork was precise.

One day, my friend, Hipolito—the only man I've

ever seen *kick* a basketball rim—told me a story about
how he went parking up on top of Scenic Mountain.
How he smoked dope and listened to *Little Joe* and
tugged at his girlfriend's bra.

I was inspired. I immediately grabbed the Spanish-
English phrase book my mother gave me for my birth-
day. After mastering a salutation, I decided to try and
talk my masseuse into a date up on Scenic Mountain.

"Como se llama?"

God she was inscrutable. Only smiles. I knew she
understood my little phrases because I was speaking
proper Spanish—the kind they speak in old Mexico
and Spain. Hipolito said my masseuse was from the
state of Guanojuato. Had some Aztec in her.

I said, damn right she's got some Aztec in her;
cheekbones for days, skin like bare copper wire. I went
overboard for this girl; this silent girl, who rubbed my
legs with Tiger Balm.

Then one day, I finally finished the short-wave
radio component of my entertainment center. I'd been
trying to talk Hipolito into sticking a parabolic antenna
up on the mountain for me. I wanted to pick up one
of those mega-watt stations out of Mexico. At first,
he refused, but all it took was a small bribe for new
sparring gloves, and he ran an antenna up to the roof
for me.

One of those crazy evangelical gospel hours was
the first program I picked up; must have been on a
Sunday.

"Me llamo Zamarillo."

"What?" I cried. "Zama...Zamarillo is your
name?"

"*Si joven. Zamarillo.*"

That's all she said, but that's all it took. We were by-god connected.

She went back to rubbing, smooth and warm, while the preacher man was wailing. God, I could feel the energy. Those poor rotting guys, they couldn't appreciate the energy in that room: Zamarillo rubbing and humming; the preacher ranting and raving. This was the by-god physical. I could feel it; burning. I smiled at my smiling masseuse, who rubbed my dead muscles. She brought me back to life, some other life that she understood instinctively, a native life. All right there in the palm of her hands. In the palm of her hands in Big Spring, Texas. And I was one blessed conduit.

"Zamarillo! Zamarillo!" I cried.

And then on day thirty-three, things were different. Let me tell you about this higher plane we (me and Zamarillo) flew to every afternoon.

The program started about 1:30, after a lunch of cafeteria surprise. Zamarillo would come in with four tubes of ointment and strip the sheets off my legs and raise my gown. I'd tune in to the 24-hour gospel ministry and raise the bed to low recline.

I concentrated on the rhythm of the preacher's voice and her fine Aztec hands. In my head I heard the drum; mental percussion—boom baba boom—keeping pace with these two naturals: a voice in the form of sound waves and her silent hands rubbing. And when I closed my eyes, the journey began and I could see my truck flying into the crater. There was something very pure about the look on my face; as I flew into the future. Zamarillo understands.

Then I'd begin to float. Not literally, but on a nice Ali Baba carpet of electrons that the preacher and Zamarillo generated as they gradually quickened their pace. I could feel my blood pumping, my heart beating to the rhythm and soon my world became hypersensitive; all warmth and gently spilling waves. Even the bed, when it started to creak, the syncopation was perfect.

I was aware of the other men, their occasional moans. But Zamarillo was quiet. Quiet like the organ pipe cactus that stood sentinel outside our window.

I felt the old schematic urge to explain to the guys where me and Zamarillo were flying. I know they knew the place; we'd all been there before. I just never thought…Let's just say the Texas Mental Health Department works in mysterious ways.

This evangelical radio phase of my spiritual reeducation proceeded for some time. Could have been months; could have been years, but I cared less as long as I was in my sweet Zamarillo's arms.

That is until the afternoon the head nurse rolled in the new entertainment system. And I do mean rockin'. This baby had the works: TV, VCR, stereo with cassette *and* turntable.

I immediately commandeered all the components for my physical therapy sessions. But the prime ingredients: evangelical radio and the Aztec rub and hum, were retained. However, it must be noted, that Hipolito's *norteño* cassettes, and the crack of Chicago Cubs baseball made for a richer experience. Even Zamarillo began to linger, often until the sun ducked behind Scenic Mountain, filling our fourth-floor room with drowsy shadows.

We climbed higher, every afternoon. Then one day I recognized a tenuous link between what I was experiencing with Zamarillo and a phase during my fourth month as supply clerk in Viet Nam. The strictly non-Marine episode when I became temporarily lost in the misty world of Mitsubishi calendar girls; the curvy Asian sirens that took me by the hand during the Tet Offensive and protected me from the screaming fragments of full metal jackets.

The memories were disturbing.

I quit talking in group.

I had a lot on my mind. Most of it magical. But that was not necessarily a good thing.

Toward the end of my psychic sabbatical, I'd stare into Zamarillo's eyes and watch her hands rubbing, rubbing; always moving with metronome consistency.

I wished the calendar girls away. "Vanish, I say! Up periscope!" I scanned the *llano*; I scanned the horizon beyond my hospital perch. Angels and demons danced two-steps and waltzes on the vapors that whistled, cartoon-like, from my unsuspecting ears.

I remained in this state of suspended animation. Then one day, I glanced at the TV over Zamarillo's shoulder. It was early in a re-run spring, and I saw Sheriff Dillon draw quick and fire a tremendous chrome-plated revolver.

A Colt .45.

Miss Kitty quivered in a corner as the bad guy, bleeding ketchup and grimace, slumped in his chair. Smoke drifted out of the sheriff's gun in backlit wisps.

Right then and there, I began to conjure my dream date: a blending of the mental boy I had become and the physical man Zamarillo had created.

"Take me to the mountain, Zamarillo. *El montonya, pronto, Zamarillo.*"

"*No joven, no ahora,*" she said. "*Anoche.*"

"*Si,*" I said, lifting her hands off my sticky thighs. "*Anoche.*"

That afternoon, after Zamarillo slipped off to prepare for our date, I rotated in my bed, cooking in the fourth-floor heat.

I was so inspired by the array of firearms presented during the afternoon reruns, that I pulled a roll of money from my pillowcase—money my parents had given me—and asked Hipolito to secure me a weapon and transportation to Scenic Mountain with drinks and sunset included.

Hipolito said he was doing something else that night.

"Come on, Hip! There's nothing going on at that Big Spring/Permian game," I explained, "except the Frito pies. I have to admit, they do serve world-class chili and chips at Ratliff Stadium."

I wasn't getting through.

"Please Hipolito; pretty please," I said, "with *mescal* on top."

He smiled at that. Shook his head, no; then took the bills from my hand.

As the hour approached, I lay in bed and listened to the blood rush to my brain. Prior to the Zamarillo rub and hum, playing linebacker against Houston Yates, smashing head-on into a running back named

Johnny Bailey, had been my most physical experience. Until I met Zamarillo.

I could feel the blood that used to fill my linebacker legs being crammed into my skull. Brain tissue, long dormant, suddenly engorged. I thought of shaving my long blonde hair so I could see the veins slowly rising, slowly etching my scalp. But I thought better of it.

I was no method actor.

Finally, as the hawks floated by my window, riding their afternoon thermals, I entered a realm previously experienced by guys with 14-pound brains in Czarist Russia. I wasn't just sensitized; I was a seismomorph.

Hipolito wheeled his primer gray Impala up to the kitchen dock and loaded me in the backseat. Waiting for me was a quart of chilled Budweiser and what this Marine considered a very inexpensive handgun. Zamarillo was sitting shotgun, wearing a *serape* with a dandy black and orange chevron motif. She and Hipolito hummed along to *ranchera* ballads as we proceeded on a slow, impressive ride to the top of Scenic Mountain; past the Prairie Dog Town and everything.

Man was I pleased—rolling with my homeboy Hip and the girl with the *manos de amor.* I snapped a crisp salute to a prairie dog sitting two-legged on the side of the road packing his pie-hole with thrown-away Corn Nuts.

Photographic memories of my mom and dad, and my wife in a purple angora sweater flashed in the blinding rays of the setting sun. I so wanted to connect; so wanted to go home. I told myself, kind of pleaded actually, come on now, no tears. No, no. Look how happy they are. Come on now."

Even with Adam and Eve leading my way; practically holding my hand…I, I.

Anyway, so Hipolito made it to the top and parked on The Bluff with the sun growing rounder and redder on the horizon. I could see my fourth floor haven at the foot of the mountain. It looked dusty, like a squat buffalo hunkered down in a bog. Sunbeams reflected willy-nilly off the crinkled aluminum I'd lined my window with for better radio reception.

"The energy," I said, caught in the moment, the fourth floor fairly pulsating in my mind. I was gathering strength for the flight.

Zamarillo crawled over the seat and on top of me. Unexpected, but very cool. From this vantage I could see the hospital, the sun, the slow curve of West Texas, and two bottomless black pupils. I pulled the *serape* over her head and threw it on Hipolito's spotless back floorboard. Her fine copper skin was alive with goose flesh.

"Let's go, Zamarillo," I said, hugging her to my chest. Hipolito twirled an imaginary lasso above the dashboard, as we commenced, leaf springs squeaking.

First, through the tunnel, past pre-natal care, past Riddler lunch boxes, Science Fair static displays, past my smoldering truck in the crater, over the land of hospital electrons, and back into the womb. I was floating with countless cheekbone generations who watched us kiss and caress, chanting to the quickening beat.

I whispered something to my angel, ran the barrel

along her spine. She never said a word when the thin red seam etched my flesh. But the mountain did. It roared back, and I was scared—scared I'd gone too far.

I watched a telltale funnel drop from a sudden wall of cloud, dipping like a bruise-colored needle. Punching holes in the desert.

I shivered inside the black torrents of Zamarillo's hair.

Finally safe.

And that is where I stayed. That is where Jehovah's witness laid me down.

Safe and sleeping in a fine leather pouch that hangs from her neck. Zamarillo's favorite powder. Bouncing in the cleave of her quiet bosom. Born-again electrons. Free to fly. Free to dance.

Like a muscle-bound Mojo.

Mother Teresa Comes to Dallas

Dallas, Texas
November 23, 1990

Morgan Wooten was finished writing his copy for the day, but wouldn't leave the office before five. Even on Friday. So, he walked up to the ever-so- tastefully appointed Neiman Marcus Catalogue Division reception area, grabbed the latest *Time*, and took it back to his cubicle. After idly scanning the magazine, he returned to an article on Mother Teresa, to a particular quotation.

"The rich are emotionally impoverished," said the Saint of Calcutta. "Only the poor know true joy."

Later that night, a young man pointed a handgun at Morgan. Life did not flash before Morgan's eyes. Rather, he saw Mother Teresa's sad smile flicker across the gunman's face, heard the flutter of angel wings beat against the roof of his late-model Mercury.

Mother Teresa had come to Dallas. But definitely *not* on Air India.

Morgan was so happy to be back in his decathlon-training groove, with a great post-grad coach at SMU, making a little mindless cash on the side with the help of Mr. Stanley Marcus. Holed up in an efficiency apartment off Lover's Lane. Holed up, off and on, with an unimaginably hot Icelandic javelin tosser named Tulia.

Life was steady. Life was time-managed to the minute: rise, run, lift, work, practice, eat, sleep. Do it again. Meets on the weekend; indoor heptathlons in the winter; full-on outdoor decathlons in the spring and early summer. But mostly practice. Lots and lots of meticulously organized running, jumping, hurdling and throwing. And vaulting. He spent way much too much time attempting to leap tall buildings in a single bound.

Tulia was proving to be pretty Viking-like in her appetites, as well. The girl went five-eight, one-fifty, and could chuck a spear out of the damn stadium, among other things. And naturally, she was ice-water blonde—the type of blonde that blinded mere Northern European mutts such as Morgan. The good news was Tulia was long way from Reykjavik. Morgan, the native Texan and her preferred protector, caught a lot of slack from this flaxen-haired goddess, and a lot more sack time than he deserved.

Morgan knew he was lucky; knew he and Tulia couldn't possibly survive the strain of their increasingly obvious incompatibility. But in this early 90s interim, what Tulia and Morgan made as a couple was always striking.

This particular Friday night, however, Morgan was alone and slumming. In torn, faded Levi's, a tight black Adidas t-shirt, black denim jacket; acting out an overconfident weekend fantasy following a shallow spat with Miss Tulia. After a melodramatic slam of the apartment door, Morgan decided what he needed right now was some smoke; a well-deserved reward for a just-completed indoor heptathlon season.

He sat idling curbside in dangerous Deep Ellum, the wanna-be SoHo of Dallas, with the windows of his four-on-the-floor Cougar rolled down, drinking semi-warm Budweiser in a brown paper bag, listening to the muffled thumps of a Zen-metal band from Seattle called Soundgarden, who were raging in a retrofitted warehouse named The Venue.

Most of the twenty-somethings milling about the sidewalk looked like mannequins. All dressed in permutations of black. They looked serious. Seriously posing, Morgan thought. Seriously full of that peculiar brand of urban angst that simply didn't exist in the small-town south Texas where he was raised. Not that he was down on all of the twenty-something Dallasites. The crack officer candidates Morgan worked with at Neiman's, they were real deal for sure; smart, witty and spirit-crushingly ambitious. But out here in the Deep Ellum alleys, *faux* was king: fake hair, fake laughter and lots of preppy and punk swagger, but not a trace of true joy, as far as he could see.

Soundgarden's set ended, and Morgan focused

on a muscle-bound amputee in a dirty Polish Solidarity T-shirt. The amputee drank from a green-label whiskey bottle and moved about athletically on his crutches.

"Wonder what he just scored?" Morgan thought, as the young man crutched his way past the car, a cellophane bag of something peeking out of the back pocket of his jeans.

Two blocks down, in the doorway of a warehouse, that was decidedly not retrofitted, sat the dude who was selling. Or so Morgan hoped.

Morgan pulled up to the curb. Rolled his window down. "Selling?" he asked.

"Come here," said the man, standing up.

Morgan saw that he was a slight-built guy, like a 10,000-meter man, and not too tall, wearing a wool cap pulled down over his ears and a navy blue Members Only windbreaker with jeans and sneakers. Inexpensive canvas sneakers.

"No, you come here," said Morgan.

The man reluctantly picked up his plastic grocery sack and walked up to Morgan's window. "You the police?" he asked, standing a couple of feet from the window. "Let's see some ID."

Morgan was surprised, then thought it a reasonable enough request. He fished his wallet out. "Here. I'm not a cop."

The man took the license and studied it, then pulled a packet of papers bound with a rubber band from his sack. "I ain't got a driver's license, but this here is real. Just got it, two days ago."

Morgan read the name on the Social Security card. "Eskar Earl Nelson," he said, handing back the card. "Is Eskar a family name?"

"No. It's just my name."

"Oh," said Morgan, looking in the rearview for police cruisers. "Say, Eskar, think you can score me some dope?"

"You looking for Ex, or white?"

"Just weed."

"I know where we can find some biscuit real fast," said Eskar. "Weed too. Let's ride."

As Eskar made his way to the passenger side, Morgan thought, this is fucking dumb, man; dumb, dumb, dumb.

But now Eskar was in the car. And so was Eskar's plastic sack. And that seemed pretty permanent. So, Morgan put the car in gear, and off they went.

He was prepared to pull over at the slightest hint of danger, but for now, Morgan was going to cruise. See if he could hang in the underworld. Eskar was going to be his escort across the River Styx. In this case, the Trinity River: a quick left under R.C. Thornton Freeway into South Dallas proper—land of broken glass and buckled pavement; lost souls and blue ladies on every corner. It all seemed very romantic to Morgan.

"You want some beer?" asked Eskar. "It's still cold. I bought it at the 7-Eleven."

"Sure," said Morgan, reaching for the paper-sacked quart of Old English 800. He took a manly pull. "Thanks, Eskar."

"Sure man, I'm good people."

"I do believe it."

Morgan was driving where no man, except idiots looking for dope, dared to drive at 1 A.M. He took another swig, then Eskar killed the bottle.

"You know Eskar, this might be a real Heart of Darkness thing."

"What you mean, heart of darkness?"

"Dude, chill. It's a book; Joseph Conrad," said Morgan, smiling at his escort.

"Stop this fucking car. Stop the car, man!" yelled Eskar, grabbing the steering wheel.

"Wait! Shit! Jesus, let go!" yelled Morgan. "Let go, man!" He slapped Eskar's fingers off the wheel and slowed to a stop next to the tiny package store.

"Why you talking about hearts of darkness and shit, man?" said Eskar. "Fuck that voodoo shit, man. I believe in Christ Jesus."

"Wait, what? I do too. Nobody's talking about voodoo," said Morgan, pleading. "It's cool. I didn't mean nothin' by it."

"What'd you say it for then," said Eskar, settling back in his seat. "Talking that bullshit."

"Hey, I'm sorry," Morgan said, looking in his side view mirror to see if he could pull back on the avenue. "Maybe this isn't going to work. That's cool."

Eskar took a deep breath, and exhaled; gave his driver a long look. "Take a right; next block," he said, pointing, his voice, back to business. "I didn't mean to go off. But one thing I learned is, don't trust no-body. Everybody's crazy. You know what I'm saying?"

"Oh yeah," said Morgan, turning from the freshly paved boulevard onto a side street lined with cars and riddled with potholes. "That's why I'm glad you're riding shotgun."

"Damn right," he said, slapping the dashboard

with his palms. "Don't no-body fuck with Eskar Earl Nelson."

"Glad to hear it."

A couple of blocks off the main drag, the streets became darker. Most of the streetlights were burned, broken or shot to pieces.

"You don't want no coke?" asked Eskar. "How 'bout ecstasy? Sell it all the time to you white boys."

"Where?"

"Clubs down in Ellum. Where them punk-lookin' boys hang out," said Eskar. "Shit, two weeks ago, this one white dude gave me five hundred bucks. Cash! He knew I could walk. But I'm good people. I don't fuck people around. Not like a nigger. Jack you up as soon as they see the cash. I brought that boy back a whole shitload of E-train."

Morgan laughed. He could just imagine the teenager, as awkward and anxious as himself, handing Eskar all kinds of cash. Then gobbling blissful fistfuls of Ex upon his return. The score, positively miraculous.

"I did Ex a few of times, back when it was legal. Loved everybody. But the hangovers were death, man," said Morgan, driving as fast as he dared, about twenty-five. "All I do now is weed. Maybe a big bag, if we can find it."

"Don't want no white, huh?" said Eskar, scratching his sparse beard.

"Coke makes my heart go pitter-patter," said Morgan. "Scares the hell out of me."

"Been there many a time," said Eskar. "Been so wired I scratched myself bloody."

"No shit?" said Morgan. "That sounds terrible."

"Man's got to learn to control the things that make him feel good."

"It's tough, though," said Morgan. "Like a horse who don't know no better than to eat himself to death."

"Exactly, my man, exactly," said Eskar, getting more comfortable, scooting down low in the seat, hanging an elbow out the window. "I seen dudes act like animals, man. Do anything to fill that pipe. Thank God I ain't never got that way."

Morgan had seen plenty of movies, and plenty of people snorting coke, but he had no experience with crack, besides shaking his head at the headlines in the *Dallas Morning News*.

"So, you looking for weed," Eskar said, fiddling with his sack. "Bound to be some weed 'round here somewhere."

"Yeah, that's my favorite. No hangover," said Morgan, driving deeper into a neighborhood that was now row after row of dilapidated frame houses. "So, what's your favorite, Eskar?"

"My favorite's ladies," he said, laughing at his own joke. "Coke ain't got nothing on a fine woman. That's the worst thing about being in the joint. Dick gets hungry, man. You'll fuck a cold piece of bread."

"I bet that's right," said Morgan.

"Shit boy, I bet you covered up in women," said Eskar. "Take a right here."

"Used to be covered up," said Morgan, although it was just bragging. "Girlfriend kicked me out."

"So that's why you out here," Eskar said. "Dick be talking back to you, ain't it?"

"Well...no," Morgan said, trying not to laugh.

"Dick's doing okay; stays pretty pumped. Lots of pretty girls in Big D."

"I hear that," Eskar crowed. "Dallas eat up with them fine women."

Morgan steered down a back street with weeds growing tall over the sidewalks. The headlights swept the asphalt, picking up glitters. Eskar told him to slow down for two men talking beside a parked car.

Morgan tensed as he pulled beside the men and stopped; felt very, very out of place as Eskar asked the men about the local weed supply. He forced himself to slouch in the seat, take both hands off the wheel and hang his elbow out the window. He snuck a peek at the men leaning in the window, then stared straight ahead.

The men, who on second look were actually teenagers, said they knew someone who had some gage, but they needed a ride.

Suddenly, Eskar was yelling, "Go on, man" he said. "Drive!"

"Who?" Morgan hesitated. "Don't they need a ride?"

"Drive, goddammit!"

"What's wrong?" said Morgan, speeding away. "I thought you said they knew where some weed was."

"Weed, hell. Didn't you see that boy's gat?" said Eskar. "They think you got cash."

"Really?" said Morgan, taking a left. The glint of an alley cat's eyes flashed from the roof of an abandoned car.

"Yeah, really," chided Eskar. "What? You ain't never done this before?"

"Not down here."

"Slow, man. Slow, slow…. Let's see if this girl know where some weed at," said Eskar. "Where's your window button, man?"

"I got it," said Morgan, gliding the passenger window.

"Hey, girl," yelled Eskar to a wide-striding young woman in a clear vinyl raincoat, a NWA T-shirt that barely contained her top, and gray sweat pants. As he slowed down, Morgan could hear the drone of traffic on the freeway. Tires clicking rhythmically on the metal grating. The sound was comforting.

"Say, baby."

She didn't stop, so Morgan rolled along beside her.

"Hey, girl." Eskar cooed, "Slow down, now. Come talk to me."

When she stopped, Morgan stopped. She leaned into Eskar's window looking puffy cheeked and strung out.

"What's down?" said Eskar. "What you holding?"

"Not a damn thing," she said. "But I know where there's some rock."

"Don't need no biscuit, baby," said Eskar, jerking his thumb at Morgan. "Homeboy's looking for some weed."

"I know a dude sells joints," she said, smacking her gum. "He right around the corner."

"Joints ain't working, baby. Boy needs at least a quarter," said Eskar, suddenly losing interest. "Let's go. She ain't got nothing."

"Do too," she said, pushing away from the window. "I know a girl sitting on a bag. But she ain't going to sell you none."

"Get yo ass in here," he said, flinging the heavy door open and made very little effort to lean forward when the girl squeezed in. "She selling if I say she is. Where she live?"

After the girl was settled, Morgan noticed the passenger seat was too far back. Tulia kept it in low recline most of the time so she could sleep during road trips. He reached under Eskar's seat.

"Hey, man," yelled Eskar, grabbing Morgan's wrist.

"The seat! The seat," he said, trying not to grimace as Eskar's fingernails dug into his skin. "Just adjusting the seat."

Eskar let go of his wrist. "Oh, sorry, man. You know," he said, then jerked forward with too much force, driving his knees into the glove compartment.

Morgan smiled at Eskar, looked at the girl in the backseat in the rearview mirror. She was looking around the interior, oblivious. Morgan reached back under the seat and helped Eskar push the seat back a little bit.

"Hey, turn it up," said the girl. "I like this song."

Morgan tried not to stare at Eskar and the girl as she explained directions. He was fascinated; tried to feel what it was these two were feeling; tried to feel true. But as soon as he thought about it—trying to feel true. What? Some lily-white punk trying to empathize; trying to be cool—he cursed himself.

Morgan turned up the volume, "You like Young MC? You ready to bust a move?"

"What you know about bustin' a move?" she said,

thumping Morgan's shoulder then, grooving side to side. "Turn it up."

"What? You think white boys can't groove?" laughed Morgan, smiling at the girl in the rearview. Her face was blank; lost in the music, keeping time with the rapper's scat. "You're right about that. Can't dance my way out a paper bag." He pulled back into traffic behind a candy red Cadillac with white walls and curb feelers. "You gonna teach me some moves?"

"Man, this shit ain't got nothing on James Brown," Eskar said. "I'll tell you that, nine times. We used to pick up a soul station when the guards didn't snitch our batteries. Old blues and shit."

"They don't have electrical outlets in prison?" asked Morgan.

"Take a left," said the girl.

"Where? Here?"

"No, naw! baby," she said. "Up ahead. One more. There you go."

"You better be taking us to some weed," said Eskar, turning slightly in his seat. "Or we gonna leave your black ass on the sidewalk."

"Old man, you all noise," she said. "I'm just try-ing to show you where some weed at, and all you do is talk shit. Take a left."

After each turn the streets got narrower and darker. After two years in the city, Morgan knew his way around downtown and Ellum , SMU and Highland Park, but this part of town was crazy complicated. Full of dead-ends and U-turns. "Damn," he said, to no one in particular. "Where we going, troops?"

The girl pulled herself up even with the front

seats. "Over there," she said, jabbing the air with her finger. "That the one."

"Where? On the left side?" asked Morgan. "That proje…That apartment building?"

"I heard you say project, boy. See, I caught you," she said, laughing. "Look see. She home. Her TV's on. I can see her through the window."

"Go on in there and go get her then," said Eskar, as the car stopped. "And tell your girl joints ain't working. My boy needs a bag."

"I heard what you said." The girl squeezed through when Eskar opened the door. "And he damn sure ain't your boy. He my boy. Ain't that right, sugar?"

"Oh, yeah," Morgan said, smiling at the girl, nodding. "Not that I could handle it."

"I heard that," said Eskar, slapping the girl's backside as she popped out on the sidewalk. "And don't be bringing back joints."

"Hell, joints are fine," said Morgan, wishing Eskar would just close the door. Even the tiny dome light felt like a spotlight out here.

"I find you some," she said, adjusting her raincoat.

"Don't be fucking up," said Eskar.

"Shut up," she said, waving him off. "Damn you grouchy."

"Back talkin', goddamn…" he said, and slammed the door. "Just bring your ass back with some weed."

Morgan pulled into the broken-up asphalt lot across the street from the three-story brick housing project. Several people mingled in the grassless front courtyard. They watched the girl approach a man in the courtyard who had just stepped out of a smashed, faded yellow van with "Party Machine" painted on the side. The girl and the man talked for a few seconds, then she disappeared into the breezeway of the complex.

"Stay here," said Eskar, opening his door. "I'm gonna see what's down with this nigger."

No shit, stay here, was all Morgan was thinking at this point. The car clock read 2:37. I ought to haul my ass, right now, he thought, as Eskar walked up to the "Party Machine" man.

"Hey, Soul, you know that crazy bitch?" Eskar said.

"I ain't knowing nobody," said the man, eyeing Eskar, then lighting a cigarette. "What you want?"

Eskar seemed to keep his distance, as if he'd recognized the man in the match's flame. "Got any coke?"

"Why you want to know?" said the man. "You might be the po-lice."

"I ain't no cop, man," said Eskar. "You know Big Daddy T? He's my uncle, man."

"Big Daddy T?" said the man, exhaling a cloud of smoke. "Old nigger, run the grocery on Grand?"

"Yeah, you know him," said Eskar, looking away from the man's penetrating stare. "Say, man, you holding?"

"Naw, man. I been rocking all day. Smoked me a whole buncha shit," he said.

A police siren, just blocks away, turned their heads, but faded quickly. "What about that bitch you riding with? What she doing?" the man asked. "Looking for Mike Stone?"

"She say she know a girl in here selling weed."

"What you want weed for?"

"Dude driving," said Eskar, nodding back to the car.

The man looked over Eskar's shoulder. "He got any cash?"

"Ain't showed me none," said Eskar.

"I find it for him."

Morgan panicked when he saw the man approaching. He knew he should drive away, but was paralyzed. He jumped when the man rapped on the windshield with his big nugget ring, then leaned in when Morgan slid open the passenger window.

"Hey, man, you got a dollar? My van's fucked up," he said, taking another drag off his cigarette. "Need some money for a ride, man."

"I don't have any money on me," said Morgan, feeling the pockets of his blue jeans. "I might have some change."

He opened the console between the bucket seats where he kept quarters for the Tollway. Then quickly closed it. His heart pounded. "I don't have any money." The man backed away without another word. Morgan was surprised, but quickly rolled up the window.

At that moment, the girl walked across the courtyard onto the street. Morgan turned the engine over and put the car in reverse. He was going to fly in the next five seconds, but Eskar waved at him to stop.

Morgan unlocked the door.

Again, the girl stopped to talk to the van man, but Eskar yelled at her, "Let's go." He paused about a second, then got in the car. "Fuck her. Let's go, man."

When they backed into the street, the girl broke

for the car. Morgan stopped to let her in.

"What you stopping for, man? Let's go!" screamed Eskar.

"Got to let this car pass," said Morgan.

Eskar nodded as a long platinum Cadillac rumbled by. "That's the Prince. Crazy Jamaican motherfucker. Dude will make you dead, man."

Eskar scowled at the girl when she ran up to his window. "Get in the fucking car, girl. Come on."

After she was inside, Morgan accelerated and quickly caught up to the Cadillac.

"Slow down, man," said Eskar. "Don't be tailing Prince. Take a left."

When they were safely down the street. He turned and put out his hand to the girl. "You got something?"

"Naw," she said. "I could a got you some joints, but you said all you wanted was a bag."

"Pull over, man."

"Where?" asked Morgan.

"Here. Right here, man," said Eskar.

They pulled into a convenience-store-turned-restaurant's parking lot and stopped. A sign in the window read, "You Buy! We Fry!"

"Why can't you drop me off at my place?" asked the girl.

"Got no time," said Eskar. "Getting late."

"We're burning daylight," added Morgan.

"Fuck you then," she said, pushing up on Eskar's seat. "I'm tired of y'all's attitude."

Eskar shoved the seat with his shoulder, knocking the girl back. "I tell you about attitude, bitch," he yelled. "How come that motherfucker you was talking to tried to pull a gun? You setting us up? I'll kick your swole up ass."

When Eskar raised his hand the girl shielded her face. "I didn't tell him nothing," she cried.

"What gun?" asked Morgan.

"Had to stick a knife in his goddamn ribs to get him off you."

The girl again tried to get out, but Eskar wouldn't budge. He pressed his weight against the seat.

"Let her out, Eskar" said Morgan. "Let's get the fuck out of here."

Eskar obliged. "I got the word on your ass," he said, as she climbed out of the car.

"Fuck your word. Ain't nobody listening to you," she said, waving Eskar off. "You gonna be dead tomorrow, anyhow. Driving around with this white boy."

"Go on! Let's get," Eskar said, shaking his head.

Morgan watched the girl in the rearview, couldn't help but smile when she shot Eskar double fingers.

"How'd you know that dude had a gun?" asked Morgan. "I didn't see a thing. Not that I would have."

"Had it in his belt," said Eskar. "He was reaching when I put a touch of my blade on him."

"I had no idea, man," said Morgan, exhaling a deep breath. "I appreciate it, Eskar."

"I told you I'm good people. I'm looking out for you," he said. Eskar smiled when Morgan slapped him high five. "I told you I was good people."

"Yes you did," said Morgan. "And now I owe you a beer."

"Save his life, and all the boy can do is buy me a beer?"

"Can't even do that," said Morgan, pointing at the car's digital clock. "Beer's done over for tonight."

"Yeah, but the good stuff's on sale 24/7," said Eskar.

Around 3 A.M., after a few more unsuccessful laps around South Dallas, Morgan and Eskar finally located the source.

They drove down a short, dead-end street with a row of frame houses on the right, and the burned-out shell of a two-story house and an overgrown vacant lot on the left. Eskar told Morgan to pull up to a house with a brand new chain-link fence. The long platinum Cadillac they'd seen by the housing project was parked in the driveway. A naked bulb lit a porch with two plastic lawn chairs and what looked to be an expensive leather couch.

"Turn out your lights, man," said Eskar. "This dude for sure is selling weed."

"Really," said Morgan. "That's that car."

"Yeah, man. This Prince's dope man. This dude's always sitting on a spleef," Eskar said, rubbing his chin, looking at the house. "That's all Prince do is blunts. That's why he so cold-blooded. Not like these hot head motherfuckers wired up and shit."

"How come we didn't come here straight off?" asked Morgan.

"'Cause I don't like dealing with these Jamaican motherfuckers," Eskar answered. "Shoot you in a goddamn minute."

"I don't need it that bad," said Morgan. "If you think there's going to be trouble...hell, let's call it a night."

"It's no thing, as long as I show'm some cash. So he know I ain't fucking with him," said Eskar, nervously looking for a way to roll his window up.

"I got cash, but I'd like to see the weed before I pay," said Morgan.

"Ten dollars, man. I got to show him something."

"All I got is a twenty."

"That'll work," said Eskar.

"Yeah, I know it'll work, but are you coming back?" he asked, then didn't wait for Eskar to answer. "Just get some weed, man. I'm tired. You're tired. And this ain't no place to be hanging out."

He handed Eskar the bill folded long ways.

"Have I messed with you yet?" asked Eskar, opening his door. "Lock this door and…. I'll be right back."

Morgan was a little surprised that Eskar didn't break and run. But then, Eskar had surprised him all night. "I have got to get the fuck out of here," he sighed. "I can just see it: 'Park Cities Man Found Dead Outside Cotton Bowl Crackhouse.'"

Morgan watched as his partner stepped into the dim porch light. "Knock on the fucking door, Eskar. Damn."

The door opened after one knock, soul shakes were exchanged, and Eskar was right back out. Walking, then hop-stepping, to the car.

Morgan rolled down the window as he walked up.

"Man's selling fifteen dollar fingers," he said. "Says ain't nobody selling no ounce of dope around here."

"Here. Here's sixty and that makes eighty," said

Morgan, handing three more bills to Eskar, who was running in place, hands on the window well. "That's five fingers and five bucks change."

"Now you talking," said Eskar, taking the bills and folding them long ways. "I'll be right back. Keep the motor running, man. No telling what these crazy motherfuckers are down for."

Eskar walked slower this time, like he was thinking about bolting. But he didn't. He went back through the gate and up to the front door.

"Atta boy, Eskar," whispered Morgan, watching as he stepped inside. "Come too far tonight."

While he waited, for what seemed like a long time, maybe sixty seconds, two men in parkas with the hoods draped over ball caps approached the car from the burned out building across the street. Morgan made them out as teenagers. As they crossed the street, Morgan slumped down in his seat. As they got closer to the car, he tried to hide between the console and gearshift, but it was useless. He knew the boys could see him, if they were looking. Morgan cursed silently when he felt the boy's weight press against the right front fender. They began to talk loudly.

"Man, I'd stick my dick in a knothole right now," said one, in a tiny voice.

"How much shit we got left?" asked the other, in an unnaturally raspy voice, as if he had been hit in the throat with a pipe.

"Nothing for nothing," said Tiny. "What, you think I'm holding out on you?"

"Chill, boyee," said Raspy. "I'm just fucking with you."

"Shit, you know Prince holding," said Tiny.

"Man won't even let you scrape the bowl for less than a nickel," said Raspy.

Morgan was still too scared to start the engine when the house door slammed open, followed shortly by a large dog's deep guttural barks, mixed with the sinister laughter of men. Morgan inched up to look out the window, hand poised on the ignition.

"Keep that fucking dog off me, man," yelled Eskar, as he jumped off the porch. A man laughed, holding the Doberman by the collar. He waited until Eskar was half way down the sidewalk, then let the dog go.

Eskar escaped through the gate just as the dog reached the end of his tether, jerking back with a dissatisfied yelp.

"Yeah, y'all have a good time," said Eskar. "Nice doing business with you." The barking dog and the men's laughter receded behind closed doors.

Eskar slowed to a stop when he spotted the boys sitting on the car.

"What's wrong brother?" asked Raspy. "Prince's Dob-i-man fucking with you?"

"Fuck that dog," Eskar said. "I'll cut him into Alpo."

The boys laughed at that. Raspy pushed off the hood of the car and stepped up to Eskar.

"Say word, man?" asked Raspy. "You holding?"

"Nothing but my dick," said Eskar, easing up to the passenger door. "Prince done cut me off. What you think that dog shit about?"

"Fuck if I know," said Raspy. "What you doing

with that knife, nigger?"

Morgan peeked tentatively over the dashboard, watched Eskar stare down one boy, then the other. Neither seemed willing to challenge. "Yeah, me and Prince be going way back," Eskar said, tossing his lock blade from hand to hand. "'74 South Oak Cliff."

Morgan felt a little safer. Eskar seemed in control. But he wished he'd skip the history lesson. As soon as Eskar opened the door he was going.

"'74!" cried Tiny. "You an old nigger ain't you. I's born in '74."

"Kimble High. Right here, baby," said Raspy. "Best pair a 2's in the city."

"Nothing but shredding the net," added Tiny.

"You can save that shit," said Eskar, lifting the door latch. "You ain't busting a grape."

When Eskar opened the door, Morgan felt naked in the harsh interior light. It was like a Q-Beam reflecting off his blonde hair and pale skin.

"Start the car, man," whispered Eskar, as he stepped inside. "Let's go."

Morgan sat up, turned the ignition, and immediately popped the clutch. The car lurched forward, hip-checked the boys, and died.

The boys regained their balance and began shouting and beating on the hood of the car. Morgan turned the engine over and was shifting when Eskar jerked him down by his jean jacket, slamming his ear into the console. Eskar's weight pressed down on top of him.

"What the fuck, man?"

The next sounds were firecracker pops and the dull shatter of safety glass.

"Hey, hey, hey!" screamed Eskar, making himself small on the floorboard of his bucket seat.

Morgan balled up and closed his eyes while bullets, and safety glass, and the boy's whoops, filled the air.

Eskar kept on yelling, "Hey! hey! hey!" in a steady involuntarily stream.

And then finally, the windshield exploded, and the shooting stopped.

Miraculously, the engine was still running, and somehow, Morgan got his right foot on the accelerator. The engine raced wildly, but the car did not move. It had slipped out of gear.

Without raising his body above the level of the dashboard, Morgan slammed the gearshift forward. The car surged and he was able to catch the clutch with his foot before the engine died and pushed the steering wheel left.

When the car bounced over the opposite street curb, Morgan rose up and jerked the wheel right. He couldn't tell where the boys were, or even if they were still shooting. He floored the accelerator, spinning the tires in the wet grass and managed to get back on the street just in time to slam into a dead-end blockade.

"Son of a bitch!" he yelled.

"Hey! Hey! Hey!" Eskar answered.

Morgan put the car in reverse and floored it. Tiny and Raspy were waiting in the middle of the road, pointing their guns like ghetto sheriffs. Morgan bent behind the seat. He had nowhere to go but right for them. Fortunately, Raspy shot over the car, and all Tiny could do was heel-kick the passenger door as the

Cougar flew by.

Morgan kept right on flying down the dark street and didn't look back until he had covered three blocks, sideswiped two cars, a telephone pole, and several trash cans on a road he would never, ever locate in his trusty MAPSCO.

"Man…man…man…I am not believing this shit," said Morgan, pacing beside his smashed-up, hyper-ticking, trim-hanging, no-windshield hunk of Mercury. Morgan had driven straight to Lover's Lane as fast as he could and parked behind his neighborhood's elementary school. Safely out of sight.

"I cannot believe this shit," he continued. "I mean there's brain-dead, and then there's Morgan Wooten. Have you ever met a dumber white man?"

Eskar was relieving himself against the school's dumpster. He zipped up before answering. "You just bitchin' 'cause your car's fucked up, man. I mean I'm sorry about what happened to your ride, you know. I'm real sorry."

Morgan stopped pacing and stared at Eskar. "Fuck it. That's what insurance is for."

"Shit, man," said Eskar. "See what I'm saying. You ain't got shit to worry about."

"You're right," said Morgan. "But I can assure you I've got more to worry about than fixing this car."

"Like what?" asked Eskar.

Morgan took a deep breath. "I don't know, Eskar. Responsibilities. It's hard to explain, but trouble is pretty relative, if that means anything to you."

Eskar stared blankly at Morgan. "So, where you live, homeboy. 'Round here close?"

"Pretty close," said Morgan. Both car doors groaned loudly when they got in. Every creak made Morgan wince.

"Where the fuck we at, anyway?" said Eskar.

"Highland Park."

"No shit," said Eskar. "I knew you was rich."

"Hell, I ain't rich, Eskar," said Morgan, softly. He started the engine. "If I was rich I'd have dealers bringing me weed faster than Domino's. This is where I live, but I'm definitely renting."

"You renting, huh," he said, looking at Morgan skeptically. "Thought you said you was living with your girlfriend."

"I am," said Morgan. "I'm renting an apartment with her."

"Say, man, let's get the fuck out of here," said Eskar, hunching down in his seat, pulling up the collar of his jacket. "Got no friends in this part of town."

"Sure you do," said Morgan, pulling out of the parking lot, turning left on Lover's. "You took care of me in the heart of darkness. I take care of you in Highland Park."

"Don't be fucking with me," said Eskar, wagging a finger at Morgan. "I told you I don't go for that voodoo shit."

As they puttered past SMU in silence, Morgan thought about rolling a joint. Smoking with Eskar. But it was 4:30 AM.

"Where you want me to drop you off?" asked Morgan, steering down the tree-lined residential streets, past million-dollar homes and manicured pocket parks.

"Sure do have some nice cribs around here," said Eskar. "This where the big money sleeps."

"From cradle to grave," said Morgan. He knew he'd probably live in a house like these, some day. It was practically his birthright. He wondered what was Eskar's birthright? Morgan could not imagine. "'Bout time to call it a night, ain't it?"

"Hell no! man. We partners. I need a woman and some biscuit," said Eskar. "I done my part. Now what you going to do?"

"I gave you two hundred bucks, didn't I," Morgan said. "Besides, I can't be driving around in this piece of crap. Windshield all blown out and shit."

Eskar's silence made Morgan nervous. He sped up, then slowed down, not wanting to speed. The frontage road was just blocks ahead. If he could just get Eskar over to one of the cheap motels off the frontage road, he'd be okay.

"Two hundred dollars," muttered Eskar, "let's go find us a party."

"Not tonight, man," said Morgan, merging on the for-once empty Central Expressway. "I've got to get home. This car is a cop magnet and I know my girlfriend's worrying. Let me get you a room up here, at the Scottish Inn. It's right up here."

"Why you all of a sudden trying to get rid of me?" said Eskar. "Like I was bad people or something?"

"I'm not trying to get rid of you, man. Please," said Morgan. "The sun's gonna be up in an hour."

"I ain't talking about tonight. I'm talking about me," said Eskar. "I need a place to stay, man. Not no fucking motel. A house, man. And a job. You know how hard it is for a two-time loser to find a job?"

"Hell, Eskar, I'm just a student, man," said Morgan, careful not to miss his exit. "I'm being straight with you. I don't know what you're good at. But you're a good man. Somebody's bound to give you a break."

"Shit," mumbled Eskar. He meshed his fingers and put them behind his head. Stared up at the soft gray fabric lining the roof.

Morgan slowed as he passed the Scottish Inn. It was on the other side of Central, the northbound side. He took the next exit, drove across the overpass, but caught a red light.

The silence was heavy.

He wanted to run the light, but didn't chance it.

"I read this article about a nun, today. Her name's Mother Teresa. She tends to all these sick people in India. She says that only the poor know true joy," said Morgan, drumming his fingers on the steering wheel. "I'm not sure I believe it."

"What the fuck you saying?" said Eskar.

"Nothing," he said, glancing at Eskar out of the corner of his eye. "Don't listen to me, man."

The light turned green.

"So this is it, huh?" said Eskar, as Morgan pulled into the parking lot of the Scottish Inn. He gathered his plastic sack off the floorboard and opened the door. "Thought we might be friends."

"We are friends, Eskar," Morgan said, extending his hand. "Come on now."

Eskar hesitated, then reached back across the seat for Morgan's hand. Their palms met and were momentarily awkward, caught between soul shake and a firm Anglo-Saxon grip. But Morgan deftly readjusted, and clasp his free hand to Eskar's, for good measure. He looked his friend in the eye, and stayed there until Eskar did the same. "Listen, man. I appreciate all your help. You saved my ass."

"It's cool, man," said Eskar, smiling, then quickly pulled away. "Say, man, gimme your phone number. Maybe you can help me find a place to live. Gonna be getting cold here pretty soon."

Morgan found a pen and an old gasoline credit card receipt in the glove compartment. He wrote his correct phone number, but changed the last two digits, then wrote a completely fictional address and zip code.

"Here's where you can find me," he said, pointing at the paper. "This is my girlfriend's number."

"All right," he said, folding the slip of paper. "Say, what's your name again?"

"Morgan."

"All right, Mo, I'll give you a call tomorrow," said Eskar, putting the paper in his jacket. "What time?"

"Not too early."

"No, no, man," said Eskar. "Round five or six. Maybe we can do something tomorrow night, or something."

"Play some pickup ball, or something," said Morgan, extending his hand again. "And I'll be thinking if I know somebody who can fix you up with a job or a house. I'm not from here, you know, but my girlfriend, she might know somebody."

"All right then," said Eskar. "Be cool, man."

Morgan's heart began to pound. He was so close.

But just as he was about to put the car in gear, Eskar turned and put his hands on the window well. "What's your name again, man. I keep forgetting."

"You know, Mo," he said, laughing at his least favorite nickname. "Morgan Wooten."

"That's right. That's right," said Eskar, with an embarrassed smile. "I'll call you tomorrow."

Morgan looked Eskar in the eye, but couldn't hold it.

"Yeah, let's talk tomorrow."

Scandinavian Airspace

Oslo, Norway
July 21, 1995

Morgan Wooten's six-foot one-inch sleekly mus-
cled frame is stretched out face down on the vast soft
emerald green infield of Oslo's Bislett Stadium oblivious to the track and field carnival swirling around him.

He does not register the steady pitter-patter of
5,000 meter men clicking off sixty-second quarters;
the high jumper's sudden silence as she lifts off the
ground; the murmuring throngs of Midnight Sun wor-
shippers packed in this elegant Old World stadium of
brick and mortar—the kind of lovely structure that's
long ago been bulldozed in Morgan's adopted home-
town of Houston.

To the casual observer he is simply resting; con-
serving his energy between the decathlon's hallmark

bursts of exertion. But in reality, Morgan Wooten is slipping away, away from the difficult task at hand.

On this second and final day of decathlon competition in Europe's most famous track and field meet— the Bislett Games—Morgan is ostensibly participating in the third of five events—the pole vault. Morgan's track and field specialty, the decathlon, includes these first day events: the 100 meter dash, long jump, shot put, high jump and the 400 meter dash. Today's events are: the 110 meter hurdles, discus throw, pole vault, javelin throw and the 1500 meter run. The first day's competition usually runs from 9 to 5. A full day for sure, but nothing compared to the grueling second day, which often runs deep into the night, usually due to complications with the pole vault.

Morgan is a veteran of these far-flung tests of strength, endurance and psychological fortitude. He is an unusually long-term member of what he calls the "International Brotherhood of Ten Men"—a highly fluid mix of about fifteen decathletes from around the world who consistently score between 7500 and 9000 points at any given meet—basically a band of terribly coordinated gypsies traveling the world in hot pursuit of the mythical grail: "World's Greatest Athlete."

Morgan has always enjoyed the exotic travel: Bangkok, Bombay, Dubai, Istanbul, Rome, London, Paris, Munich, Prague, Moscow, Oslo and Eugene, Oregon make up the "Dazzling Dozen" decathlons on the International Track & Field Federation schedule. And he has grown quite fond, over the years, of the isolation and solitary dedication involved in mastering ten different disciplines. But all things weaken and fray with extended use and that's exactly what Morgan's body has been telling him this season.

Plus, decathletes don't make much money. And that's a pretty big problem for a man married to Madeline Nave, formerly of San Saba, Texas, and always heiress to the Nave pecan fortune. Yes, much to his wife's chagrin, a professional thinclad's earning potential is significantly less than his more celebrated colleagues in the world's major sports: soccer, football, basketball and baseball, tennis and golf. And according to his most recent calculations; a spreadsheet requested by his "only curious" father-in law, Morgan has generated, over the span of his career, approximately $900 a month in prize winnings, USOC stipends, and zero endorsements. Not one. The theory being that only Olympic gold medal winners such as, for instance, Bruce Jenner and Dan O'Brien make the Wheaties Box; not telegenic, affable eighth place finishers, at the '92 Barcelona Games, such as Morgan.

At this stage in his career, Morgan understands the mechanics of his trade intuitively. His muscle memory is finely tuned. But, instead of visualizing correct vaulting technique, like he ought to be, like he used to, Morgan prefers, these days, to slip into a kind of personal cocoon. Creating fantastic sex loops—in the middle of a track meet, mind you—starring himself, as the World's Greatest Athlete, and Fabulous Fatima, the Finnish Javelin Lass.

He's been watching the actual, the real live Fatima, all day. Watching her cut those ice-blue eyes at him. Stretch and preen. Cavort along the edges of the javelin apron. He admires her flawless complexion and deep summer tan. Her cute platinum ponytails. Her buxom density in a world of ever-diminishing body fat.

And with Fatima in mind it's easy for Morgan to blow off the normal routine of studying his rival's progress. So while the next vaulter, Dezø de Wit, a half-insane Dane, who fancies himself some kind of "heavy metal" Ten Man, roars to the crowd, Morgan playfully kicks his toes into the turf; tries to pull up; get right, but quickly aborts. He'd much rather lounge on Fatima's imaginary pillows than pay attention to a bunch of Danish theatrics.

Not that he doesn't need to get serious about this next vault. He is currently in third place with three events to go. And if he does somehow manage to vault four meters-three, he'll place in the money for the first time this year. Maybe even make a reporter take notice. And not just the stat geeks at *Track and Field News*. Maybe *Sports Illustrated*. Or a full-blown feature in *Esquire* or *GQ*. Who knows? Once, before the Barcelona Olympics, he was photographed for the cover of *Esquire*, but got cropped.

So why is Morgan dreaming?

Why can't he get up off the gorgeous Norwegian turf and get to work? Vault four meters three? Throw a javelin 200 feet? Run a 4:50 fifteen hundred, pick up ten grand, and call it a night. Why is he lying there, rehearsing lines on a Finnish chick he's never even been formerly introduced to? Why is he not calculating his own, and his opponent's, on-going and potential point totals? Like he used to. Is it because he can't justify a coach anymore? Is it because he's been doing this stuff forever and now a coach is simply fiscally irresponsible overhead?

No, the problem is fantasy Fatima. She's back in charge. Slowly pulling the straps of the ice blue satin babydoll from her wide soft shoulders. Which makes Morgan want to back up, rewind the video spooling in his mind's eye, and check it out again. Luxuriate in the dark, pixel-sharp images sliding across the back of his eyelids.

Morgan remains motionless. Tries to regain his footing in Finnish fantasy. Snug in his shiny Lycra bodysuit of metallic blue. Swaddled in tobacco-colored flannel and canvas coveralls—all the gifts of Joji Dingong, the designer at Nike; a tiny wisp of a Filipino with a brilliant grasp of the body in motion. A man who, Morgan is pretty sure, has a crush on him. Which is cool since he hasn't made Nike's freebie list since '92. But Joji always makes sure his fair-haired boy is looking tight.

Morgan writhes in the grass. His fast twitch muscles losing potency by the minute. Lost inside his headphones—a soundtrack of tasteful Scottish trance washing over him in cascades of swelling synthesizers and drum machine beats. His mouth turns up in a barely perceptible smile, the nagging guilt held at bay for the moment, as he plunges deeper inside a pure white stage set where Fatima is waiting on a big round bed. Soft-focus close-ups as she lets down her long blonde hair; the lips part; hands moving over plentiful curves. Taut ropes of muscle rippling beneath her toned skin; all manner of rhythmic flipping about on a pile of snowy down comforters.

His character speaks. "Are you glad you came?"

"Ya," she says, then kisses him.

After the kiss, Morgan rolls over on his stomach, a look of utter junkie peace spreading across his face.

And then, the very loud, very annoying sound of public address jolts him rigid. The Voice commanding—first in Norwegian, now in English: "Morgan Wooten, United States, decathlon pole vault, third and final attempt, 4.3 meters.

"Dammit," he says, guts instantly cramping. "Maybe it's time to…."

He pushes up from the soft grass and pirouettes into a lotus position. "All right already," he says, hugging his knees to his chest, pretending to stretch. He loosens the hold on his legs slightly and stares at his crotch.

"Nice going, freak show," he says, squeezing his legs shut, shaking his head. "Nice wood." He closes his eyes tight and tries to focus.

Where are we?

Bislett.

What do we need to do?

Hit 4.3.

How we going to do it?

Bend the pole. Bend the damn pole.

"Come on," he says, jumps up and jogs to his pole case. "Let's get right. Let's go! Time to fly, baby."

He trots to the space he's commandeered for himself, a backstretch corner of the stadium largely away from prying eyes, and gingerly steps through the detritus of his trade—huge Nike duffels stuffed with every conceivable track and field accessory-tape, spikes, distance shoes, throwing shoes, discus, shot, javelin, compression shorts, ball caps, shades, Ace bandages, water bottles, Gatorade, more tape.

Sticking out from underneath two of these bags, he finds his lucky pole. The one he cleared seventeen feet with last week in Moscow. He pulls the super-hip, high-tech, polycarbon black matte Gravity Crusher out of its aluminum travel tube and walks it down the springy red runway. He lifts it up and high steps twenty meters, pumping his legs, lifting his knees high to loosen the lactic acid, then stops at the edge of the pole vault runway.

"Got one more in you?" he coos to the pole. "Just one more," he says, then lightly kisses the grip, which makes him feel very silly. But what the hell? It worked in Moscow.

The bowl of the stadium surrounds him in stereophonic clamor; the sound of the world's richest, most prestigious non-Olympic meet—claps and shouts and chanting; all of it punctuated by second-long shrieks of compressed air. People packed shoulder to shoulder from front row to back. So different from meets in the States where the best you can hope for is a clump of noisy family and friends. All this enthusiasm, all this genuine joy, thanks to a man called the "Flying Finn" Paavo Nurmi, the legendary distance runner, who won nine Olympic golds, in Antwerp, Paris and Amsterdam, and since 1920, all of Scandinavia is wild for the sport.

And man, does Morgan love it; soaking up these people, this festival atmosphere. He absolutely adores this scene; his hulking pack of Ten Men from crazy countries like Mozambique and Belarus, as well as the traditional track powers: England, Russia, Germany and Jamaica. This itinerant life of travel and training, of personal bests one week and agonizing DQ's the next. This life of monkish seclusion in the fall and winter when every lift, throw, jump and run; every calorie, every liter of liquid is accounted for in log of military precision. And then the summers of willy-nilly meets, scattered across the globe from the steamy tip of Southeast Asia to the polar fringe of northern Europe. Nobody ever guessing that the nice boy from Texas, the one who's so enthusiastic, but who rarely wins, is really just a Daddy-subsidized dilettante; a man whose wife, parents and in-laws all wish he'd grow up, come home, and get a real job.

But they have no idea how much I love this, he thinks. This is who I am. All of it. Everybody. The fans. The sprinters, the weight men, the jumpers, the distance girls. All of 'em. Hell, even the suits.

Man, look at'em, he thinks, chalking the end of his pole with streaks of white. He laughs at the sight of a huge shirtless Viking man tossing his baby boy high in the air. The Royals up in their box waving to the locals like good monarchs should. Everybody out here enjoying the show, drinking their lager. Checking out the fast dudes and the skin-tight baby dolls.

Just loves it. Loves how it's cooler here in July than Houston in December. Loves how this North Sea track has the same thick, salt air as the ones on the Gulf Coast. The small town cinder tracks. The dark-skinned places where he grew up running and jumping and throwing; places with names like Victoria and Palacios and Ganado. He's right at home. And all alone; and he just wishes somebody; anybody, besides his dad, loved it as much as he does.

He claps the excess chalk from his hands into little poofs that sparkle and fall to the ground. Rail thin Luther Gray glides past, warming up for his 800-meter final. When their eyes meet, Morgan shoots him a down low peace sign.

Ol' Luther, the man with the reddest eyes in Africa; a four-time Olympian from Ghana and possessor of the finest smoke on the circuit; a man who Morgan has spent more time with this season than in their previous ten combined. A man whose father, Dr. Jedediah Gray, knew Malcom X. A man who's taught Morgan a thing or two about priorities, about why it's important, crucial, for a man to keep running till he can't run any more.

He waves at Amy Acuff, a fellow Texan, who's putting on her sweats after successfully high jumping 6'4"—a monster sky. Yeah, hi Amy. You tasty-looking beanpole. Yeah, I know. I get it. No love for the unranked; for the unendorsed.

He drops his pole beside the runway, and catches the attention of the blue-blazered official sitting next to the vault box, the bulk of his big Norse body about to explode his too-small plastic folding chair. The official makes an impatient "let's-get-going motion" with his ballpoint pen. Morgan mouths "one minute" as he spreads his feet wide on the grass and stretches his groin from side to side. The official nods and holds up one finger.

Morgan grimaces. That's right, I'm not bringing down the big appearance fees anymore, he thinks, mouthing "thanks" to the official. But you will respect the former Bislett champion. It's been a couple of years, but you will let me stretch.

He swivels his torso from left thigh to right and around. Spots the real live Fatima letting loose a massive heave. Her javelin arcs gracefully through the air. "Oh my goodness," he says, as it stabs perfectly into the ground, then sighs, at the sight of Fatima's bobbing backside, running away from him. Typical, he thinks, another fantasy bursting into flame.

He rises up from the groin stretch to find the giant official staring at him. "Okay, Mr. Man. I'm coming," he says, grabbing his pole. He goose steps a few meters to his tape mark at the back of the runway. Toes the imaginary line. Cracks the joints in his neck, ankles, back and right wrist. "Come on!" he hisses, acknowledging the ever-observant Dezø de Wit with a tip of his chin.

You're going to let Johnny Rotten, beat you? Is that right? Fuck that.

He lays the pole on his right shoulder, lays it in the perfect pole vault groove between his 19–inch neck and the collarbone he separated against Sul Ross. He closes his eyes, tight. One deep inhale…and out. Inhales again. Soaks up the clapping crowd. "Speed, drive, lift," he says. "One time. One time."

He bounces the tip of the pole off the runway a couple of times. Torques the grip with his hands. Stares at the veins running the length of his arms like tributaries drawn on parchment. He lifts the pole high in the air. Takes a last, deep breath, and then, he's off. Sprinting toward the box, gaining impressive speed; plants cleanly, and vaults into Scandinavian airspace.

On the way up, Morgan feels a second jolt,

different from the impact jolt, but nevertheless, executes a flawless handstand and flips unhindered over the bar.

When Morgan looks down, he sees that the pole has broken into two jagged pieces, somehow held together during the vault by yards of athletic tape. He can't believe it, but doesn't panic, either.

Just kick it, he's thinking. *Kick it!*

He's thinking something else entirely when that jagged edge impales him between the soft tissue of his sphincter and scrotum. Impales him in front of thirty-five thousand Norwegians and a worldwide television audience.

No fucking way, is his first, and only, thought.

And then nothing at all.

Just pain. Searing, gutbucket pain, as he lays buried in the soft cushions of the vaulting pit. Every breath in the stadium sucked, held. Waiting.

And after a few seconds of thrashing, he firms his grip on the bloody fragment and starts pulling. And yelling.

And yelling and pulling.

And when the pain starts feeling like a weird kind of answered prayer; he knows he's not going to die. He just needs to pull. Eyes closed tight in the dark. Eyes closed tight to the pain. *Don't look. Keep'em closed. Just keep pulling.*

And when Morgan Wooten finally does yank that ungodly splinter clean out of his ass, the crowd goes wild, CNN goes live, and things change considerably.

Mr. Elmo Comes a Krushing

Agana, Guam, US Protectorate
March 1, 2000

I have contraband in my butt. I have contraband in my girlfriend's butt. And it's fundamentally uncool.

You know, it just is. No way around it.

And I've got to get my story straight, because when the need to hire an attorney arrives, I'll need to tell her the truth. Not this fictional crap I've been making up to cover my ass with family, friends and business associates.

The truth.

Oh, and did I mention that I'm a little freaked out about muling two keys of uncut Loatian heroin. Because if I didn't, I'm sure you can look into my eyes (yeah, the one with pupils the size of saucers) and see that something is terribly wrong. Although, if you'd heard me talking my girlfriend into it, over the past three days, you'd swear I was a pro at this stuff. No problem. Piece of cake. No way in the world U.S. Customs, or anybody else with "busting" authority, is going to look twice at the attractive pair of young Americans on their way home from a business holiday in Manila—the former "Pearl of the Orient."

I'm looking at Carly and everything's cool. She looks like she's asleep, even though she's probably faking. We've been on the plane four hours; Philippines AirLines flight 482, Manila-Houston, with a re-fuel in Guam. Lucked out this time and got one of PAL's new 747's. Much better than the Viet Nam-era DC-10's I've had to endure over the past five years. We're upstairs with two big gray business-class seats to ourselves. All swallowed up in leather, with movie on-demand, and a small squadron of PAL flight attendants to see to our every need. We've already been served one meal and a snack, which sucks, because we can't eat, or drink. Anything. On a seventeen hour flight.

Which is why Carly may be faking. Because she was so bummed about not getting to booze and gorge like we usually do on these flights. But she did fall asleep watching *Fear*, which stars Marky Mark. So she probably isn't faking because she *loves* Mark Wahlberg. Normally, there's no way she sleeps with Marky Mark in the house. Normally, she orders more champagne and giggles at the sight of the Calvin Klein boy's quivering, cut-up abs.

So, I'd say she's definitely asleep. Which is amazing

since she and I each have one kilo of uncut Laotian heroin lodged in our guts. Which is why I can't even think about sleeping.

And Carly can?

Why is it that she can sleep while I'm doing the bug-eyed freak-out? I suspect it is because she is genuinely hard, and I am not. I suspect that Carly is instinctively confident in her drug mule role and I am only putting myself in harm's way. I am the one who dreams this shit up, but that doesn't mean I am in any way qualified to participate.

Carly's a player. Born and bred.

I used to be a player. A football player. Track dude; decathlete. But it's been over ten years since I smashed a man with malice aforethought. And now that I'm no longer stuffing holes, or hurling javelins, or vaulting the equivalent of small buildings, I've turned into something else entirely.

Something slightly unrecognizable, like that muscle-bound Mojo I used to babble about.

Thirty more minutes until we calmly deboard the plane during the scheduled refueling stop in Agana, Guam, United States Protectorate. And here's my fantasy: me and Carly, my seatmate; the unbelievably cool, blonde-haired, green-eyed Master of Accountancy, we throw the blankets back from our massively reclining seats and walk directly to our respective bathroom stalls in PAL's posh new Mabuhay! Club and proceed to flush out of our healthy, young, non-descript American bodies, twelve balloons. Twelve balloons, each filled with uncut Laotian Poppy Krush.

That's heroin for those of you in the DEA.

Only nobody clears Customs in Agana.

The reality is, we clear Customs in Houston, and Houston is eleven hours away. And I've got busy brain something fierce.

Maybe I should try fake sleeping too because this sucks. Just like the last six months of my life, which has, through some fault of my own, but definitely not all, gotten significantly off-track. And now I've gotten Carly directly involved. Not that she hasn't known from the start about the unbelievable bind I'm in.

We've been going together for about five years— so she knows it all. The entire sorry saga of selling my cigar company to these big Internet kingpins out of Knoxville, which should have been my first clue. But I bit on it, boy. The whole Knoxville rich guy shtick. And man, did it cost me some pain and suffering.

His name was Crazy Eddie Washburn, and he flew me non-stop Houston-Knoxville. Brand new Brazilian jet. Very professional. Eddie's company, Rocky Top Tobacco, had agreed to buy my five Filipino cigar brands for their Internet mail order business and I was coming in from Houston to seal the deal. Had my father's blessing. Totally legit.

Anyway, long story short, Eddie picks me up at the Knoxville Airport in a Bentley. The guy's my age, probably thirty-three, and swear to God, he's driving a jade green Bentley around in the foothills of the Smokey fucking Mountains, and he offers me seventy-five thousand cash for the international rights to my five brands and all the cigars in my warehouse in Texas.

"Or," he says.

And I'll never forget the crazy-looking smile this guy shoots me as he's hunting for his University of Tennessee fight song CD; these guys are huge UT fans, they pull their yacht right up to the stadium on game day. Can you believe that nouveau crap, floating a 70-foot yacht on some TVA lake? Jesus, man; I was so out of control. And I'm saying this to myself, at the time, saying no way are these guys legit. But I still go along with it because I'm so desperate to sell my company because my dad's been subsidizing the whole cigar thing for the past four years to the tune of $600,000 in the hole and now he's liable for the whole nut and that ain't going to work because we sold literally millions of dollars of cigars in '97 and '98, but the market went to hell with the dot.com crash and no way am I asking Dad to cover my no-cigar selling ass. Not for a minute. Not six hundred K. Not a dollar.

So anyway, Crazy Eddie offers me three million shares of Rocky Top's parent company, an Internet search engine based in San Antonio, that's trading at $35 dollars a share on the NASDAQ. And this is the Fall 1998, the absolute peak of the Internet stock insanity, which closely paralleled the hand-rolled cigar insanity, of which I was a prime beneficiary, seeing as we were the only company in the US importing cigars from the Philippines.

Anyway, so I do it.

I take the stock, which as of today, is worthless, delisted Pink Sheet junk. No liquidity, no worth. But that afternoon, with Crazy Eddie beaming, Charlie Daniel's fiddling on the stereo, and me sharing nips of Jack Daniel's from the guy's secret Bentley console flask and doing the math in my head, which looks like $10.5 million gross, which probably nets out, minimum $1 million, and I take it.

My gut says absolutely not. Like when I agreed to ship 40,000 cigars to a Nike golf club rep in Providence, Rhode Island, who started his own distribution company selling cigars to golf courses, and I send the guy 1600 boxes of Fighting Cock, sight unseen, get paid for the first 800 up front and never see another dime. I'm on the phone with the guy every day for a month and the check is always in the mail.

Same deal.

I knew Eddie's stock option deal wasn't right. But that's what happens when you coat your gut with sour mash whiskey and sit on the 50-yard line for the Tennessee-Georgia game surrounded by the co-ed equivalent of Charlie's Angels. Nothing but Volunteer Orange and Rocky Top yelling. Crazy Eddie plain hooked me. And if it hadn't been him, it would have been the next buyer in line because I had to get out. Get off the family dole, square up with Dad, and get on down the road with Carly.

Because Carly's the real deal. Smart, hot and work ethic for days. The girl keeps a 4.0 in accounting, works full-time for this absolute money-printing boss, who pays her huge hourly bucks because she's the only woman he's ever hired who can keep up with him. And she's all over the intangibles; parties like an absolute Trojan.

You should have seen her bouncing down the jetway two days ago, at Ninoy Aquino International

Airport, on the teeming, fetid canal side of Manila. No-bra, no sleep, big curvy hips all spilling out of these low-slung jeans. And of course, I'm towering above all these happy, smiling thronging Filipinos. We're all kind of bobbing up and down behind these thick iron security bars, and I'm waving and hollering like some kid at a calf scramble. Man, was I glad to see her. You know, halfway around the world; in bad trouble. I hugged her hard.

And about the only thing a body can do, to fight the jet lag, is drink and fool around. Especially if you're turning around in 48 hours. And that's all we did. In the room, by the pool. Hell, one time we did it under the hotel helipad. Monsoon coming down all around. Seriously, I can't keep my hands off her.

Anyway, so we walked over to the Makati Hard Rock for a hangover cheeseburger the afternoon before we left, but the rest of the time we pretty much stayed naked in the room and double-stuffed the Krush. Mylar on the inside. Synthetic rubber on the swallowing side. No way that smack was busting loose in my baby's guts. That's all we did, eat, drink, watch SkyTV and stare. At those fruit-colored balloons. Until it was time to eat 'em and go to the airport.

And I got so nervous I had to have her one more time after the bellman came up to get our bags. But Carly's cool. She knows that's the only thing that calms me down. And even then, she doesn't act like it's a chore. She's kissing me like she means it. Even when I was on my knees, pressing my face into her ass so she couldn't see me weeping like a titty baby, getting her new Victoria's Secret panties all wet. That's the woman you lay it down for.

Carly, Carly, Carly.

Anyway, I'm checking her out. Right now. Feeling her pulse and kissing her cheek. She's got her hair up in a ponytail. It's sticking out the back of her Astros ball cap. She's all cuddled up. I don't know how the hell she escaped from New Caney, Texas, but I'm thanking sweet Jesus that she did. I need saving.

I ought to wake her up and tell her—"I'm saved, baby!" Find the airport chapel in Guam and quit living in sin. But it's way too early to be celebrating.

Really, it's perfect timing for her jet lag to kick in. And when it does for real, when the jet lag hammer comes down for good, she might sleep all the way to Houston. I'll see if she wants to walk around a little bit when we get to Agana. But I doubt it. Not the way she's snoozing.

And don't worry, I'm checking her breathing. She's not nodding. She's not OD'ing. She's sleeping. All racked out with a kilo of pure death sitting in her stomach. Waiting for a pinprick to leach the poison out. Me too, I ate twelve and a little extra one with the scraps. And if it's my time, I need to go. The man can call me up at a moment's notice because I know my time's been privileged—many gifts, many advantages.

But not Carly. She's had to fight a helluva lot harder for a whole lot less than I've been given. And the only reason she's sitting here is because the guy I handpicked in Houston to take over muling for me, after this one last shipment, got hijacked in a Subic Bay titty bar.

You know, fucking typical of my managerial skills. I let the guy (I've known him ever since I got in the cigar business) out for one night of R&R, after we fix this whole too-short cloth liner fiasco and understand that we're going to have to mule two kilos in our stomachs and crap it out when we get to Houston. This is two nights before we're supposed to leave, and some bar girl down in Olongopo slashes the stupid fuck's face with a broken San Miguel bottle.

Ten years I've been coming to the Philippines, ten years, and nothing, not one time do I have any, not one single problem. Trust me, if the bar girl is willing, she can handle just about anything.

Which makes me laugh because Carly would so cut me off if she heard me talking that bar girl smack. The first time we came to Manila together I took her down to me and my dad's favorite hangout, this place in Makati called the Purple Parrot, and not five minutes into it, Carly's throwing down with the first girl who's tries to feed me popcorn. She bitched slapped that girl off the barstool and never looked back. The patrons thought it was some kind of male fantasy skit. Everyone hollering and throwing popcorn at'em on the floor. I was laughing too, until she clocked my ass with a closed fist.

Carly's *fuerte*, baby. Fucking *fuerte muchacha*.

So anyway, there are *no* problems with *any* bar girls in the Philippines. Ever. They need the money, and if you're cool, that's it. So I don't know what hand-picked employee said, or did, to this chick, but they still haven't finished stitching him up. The cut was so deep, and he lost so much blood, they had to MediVac him from Subic Bay, (which, ironically enough, used to have one of the best triage units in the world during Viet Nam, but no more) to some metro hospital in Manila. And I could give a shit if he stays the rest of his life in the PI. Serves him right; dumb-ass punk could have turned this Krush deal into a nice big payday.

So I leave my stitched-up mule moaning in this stuffy ass hospital room down on Taft Avenue, down where General MacArthur used to hang out during World War II, and I'm back in my room at the New World with a half-kilo of heroin sitting under a room service omelet cover.

Normally, forty-eight hours before I leave, I'd be getting my game face on; walk over to the lobby of the Manila Pen, across the street, you know, acting the part of the earnest young American entrepreneur. Drink a few San Miguel's; maybe order some fresh mango and smoked fish. Shake hands with the resident oligarchs. Compliment them on the cut of their *Barong Tagalogs*. But no, mule boy goes and gets his head slashed, and I can't swallow *twenty-five* 2-gram balloons. At least I don't think I can, after I scatter'em across the entire width of my King Size bed. I'm thinking, no way. I've got to call Carly.

So, it's four AM Houston time, but she says she's up studying, and while I'm waiting for her to finish downloading her WebCT class notes, I already have Plan B in place—I'm going to get this one half-American, half Filipina bar girl down at Miss Brunei's, this strip club by the bay, to mule with me.

Carly hears this and she's like, you're such a dumbass.

And I'm like, yes, that's true, but why?

She says because there's not a single bar girl in the

Philippines who looks over twelve.

And I say, yes, but the Customs guys think I look like a respectable young G.I. with his new Filipina bride. I'll go get a jarhead haircut and some Army Surplus fatigues. It'll be perfect.

See when you're an American, traveling overseas, especially a young American, all you have to do is look the part. Whatever part you want to play. That's why I wear lightweight sport coats and a tie when I travel. People don't question me. They take one look at me and figure I've got a meeting with the Tondeña Rum people or *the Asian Wall Street Journal.* The last thing they're thinking is drug mule.

I can tell you like that story, she says. Hang on a second.

And I'm like, which story? And I can tell she's a little loopy from cramming for her Non-Profit Finance test. But mainly, she hates when I go to the Philippines without her, which I've done exactly once in the past three years.

Yeah, she says, Sweetie. Just buy me a ticket and let's do this thing.

And I totally know at this point that there's no use arguing. So I tell her to go down to Balloon and Novelty across the street from the Randall's over there on Shepard and Westheimer, and buy a gross each of Mylar balloons and the highest density synthetic rubber balloons. "And if Philippines Customs asks questions, tell'em your bringing the balloons for your nephew's fiesta," I say. "I'll get you a business-class seat and bring your big hot booty to Manila."

She loved hearing that. And she brought the

balloons too, even though I told her she wasn't going to have time to do that; take her non-Profit final *and* catch a 2 o'clock flight. But she did. Because this woman is organized, unlike my dumb ass, who nonetheless, has managed to smuggle five, of the scheduled six, kilos of Krush into the United States sight unseen. All of which has to do with the fact that I've been completely disconnected physically with the previous five shipments because the heroin has been liquefied and applied to the Ikat textile liners that I wrap the Fighting Cock and Double Happiness cigars in. It's been beautiful. Perfect. And I *did* come up with this plan. Plus, I found the Laotian chemist who makes the Krush.

But that doesn't explain what I'm doing on a PAL flight to Houston with a quarter kilo of smack in my rump. So I guess I better. Explain. If that's possible.

Okay, so you know my Tennessee connection with Crazy Eddie. But there's another guy in Tennessee who does not think I'm charming, clever, or funny. He's a country-ass loan shark named Mr. Elmo—good god will I never forget Mr. Elmo.

But he's not a loan shark, exclusively. What he really is, is the Law West of the Appalachians. Mr. Elmo pretty much controls all contraband running through the Tennessee mountain slot: drugs, moonshine, gray market cigarettes. And nobody, dead or alive, owes him money. And unbeknownst to me, Eddie, Mr. Rocky Top Internet impresario, owed him six hundred grand. That's Mr. Elmo's MO. If he makes somebody dead who owes him money, he goes after the dead guy's living partner to pay.

I'm that guy. The partner.

Anyway, so Mr. Elmo.

Mr. Elmo made Eddie dead.

And Mr. Elmo may look like he just crawled out of some Dollywood cave, but he's an excellent businessman. He's six-foot five and three hundred and fifty plus. Probably four hundred. He wears nothing but Dickie's brand overalls and a brown 40X beaver Stetson. And walking shoes. Not steel-toed Red Wings like every other jobber in the hills, but all-white Etonic walking shoes. He could not sound more stereotypically hillbilly. But I understand positively, that he will kill me without remorse. Just like he killed my partner, Eddie, who offered Mr. Elmo shares of the same Internet search engine stock in trade for his debt.

Mr. Elmo was not amused by this offer. Mr. Elmo is not a day trader. He's a businessman who deals in cash. American dollars. Period. And that's why Eddie's dead.

I respect that. And Mr. Elmo knows that I respect, both him, and his enterprise.

He listened very intently when I explained my proposal to make good on my partner's debt. I had the cigar box props. I explained how this Laotian chemist friend of mine, who I'd met at a cigar dinner at the Oriental Hotel in Bangkok, had perfected a way of suspending heroin in liquid. I explained how we would dip the cloth liners that wrap my cigars, into the liquid heroin. That the tobacco would mask the heroin's odor. I told him how my company, Splendid Seed, was a legitimate, on-going import/export concern with an excellent track record with U.S. Customs and the Bureau of Alcohol, Tobacco and Firearms.

We were eating breakfast in a Mr. Elmo-sized booth at the Waffle House outside of Big Bone Cave off 70 south in east central Tennessee. Mr. Elmo pulled out a frighteningly sharp Buck knife and cut a slice of plug tobacco, while I ordered my third coffee.

"Six weeks," he said.

I told him I needed six months, no more, no less. I pulled out a detailed printout of the plan. One shipment of 62,500 cigars in 2500 boxes per month shipped to six different wholesale candy and tobacco distributors: Stevens and Pruett in City of Industry, California; Great Plains in Huron, South Dakota, who handle the Indian casinos in that area; Rothman in Brooklyn, Holt's in Philadelphia, J.R.'s in Whippanny, New Jersey, and Thompson in Tampa.

Mr. Elmo ate his eggs with his plug in place. Drank his coffee, ate his grits, biscuits, everything. Never spit. Nothing.

So this was extra-serious business. I was trying to be cool and present this guy with a carefully crafted business plan. And he listened. He was not disgusting. He did not smack, or slobber. He listened. And I figured, after he was finished listening, he was going to take me down to the Big Bone Cave and shoot me, and I'd have to run, and he'd shoot me in the Waffle House parking lot and stuff me in the grease trap and that would be that.

"Nobody gets six months to pay me back," he said, then took a swallow of sweet tea from a tumbler the size of a small oil barrel.

I told him I understood. But nevertheless, I didn't want to raise suspicions since the proposed shipment of 15,00 boxes/375,000 cigars in the first six months of 2000 would represent more than Splendid Seed had sold in all of 1999. And besides, wouldn't the margin on a single kilo of Krush be sufficient to pay off the $600,000 Eddie, and now I, owed him.

"What do you know about margins?" Mr. Elmo asked.

"What I hear on *The Sopranos*," I said.

Thankfully he laughed. He knew I was serious. Trying to do my best. I was wearing pressed khakis, a white, long-sleeved shirt and tie. My hair was cut short and combed. No gel. Just combed. I spoke with conviction about how UT had signed the best high school running back in the country from Decatur, Georgia. Not the University of Texas. The real UT.

"All right, hoss," he said.

And I about jumped out of my seat I was so relieved.

"I hear what you're saying about them Custom's boys," he said, wiping his chin with an unlikely daintiness. "They get mighty suspicious, unless their pocket's full. You got anybody paid off?"

"No sir," I said, looking straight into his poker face. "That's why I need six months. So they won't suspect."

"And you think you got them fooled?"

"Yes sir, I do."

When he started nodding and wiping his chin and looking like he'd finished with breakfast, I reached across the table to shake his hand. He kept my hand hanging there over my hashbrowns and ham steak for a second, but then he shook it. Looked me in the eye and gave me a firm grip. And I thought, this isn't much different from the cigar deals I've brokered. It's just higher margins on a different kind of luxury consumable. And totally illegal.

We walked out to the parking lot. It was one of those steel gray March mornings, cool and damp, and when I saw Mr. Elmo waving goodbye to me in the rearview mirror, I thought I might make it. If I keep my head down, work hard, attend to every conceivable detail and be willing to troubleshoot at a moment's notice, I might get this deal done and get on with the rest of my life. And maybe stow away a little money to boot.

But the money didn't matter. As long as I made enough to keep Mr. Elmo happy and pay off my dad's debt, I was golden. That's what I was thinking. I could coach ball at some little rural high school outside of Houston and Carly could get a job with Arthur Andersen, and we'd be happy.

So, now we're taking off from Guam. I tried to wake Carly up when we landed, but she didn't budge. I mean she kind of grunted, in a good way. Not in an "I'm dying'" way. She looks fine. Color's good. Breathing seems normal.

I've never done heroin. I have no idea how people react on the stuff, except what I've seen in the movies. And she's not bleeding from her nose like in *Pulp Fiction*, when Uma Thurman snorts John Travolta's heroin by mistake. She looks fine. She's facing me in the seat. Propped up on her hip. I made sure she's got plenty of pillows under her head and the blanket is pulled up tight. I mean, honestly, it's like she's having a good sleep. But I ought to call a flight attendant.

I've been that jet lagged before. I used to sleep sixteen hours straight, the times after I'd take the 17-hour flight from Houston and get to Manila at 6 A.M. and then work all day. As soon as the sun went down I'd crawl up to my little condo-tel in Makati and sleep straight to eight the next morning. I'd do it every time.

You know, maybe Carly's going to a better place, and I'm going to hell. Three hours from now, the Customs guys aren't going to give a damn if I'm wearing pressed khakis and tie. They're going to hustle my sorry ass to the airport jail and Carly to the morgue. But I can't start thinking that way yet. She's still breathing.

I can't believe this shit. I don't even recognize myself. My life. It's like I'm floating in some parallel universe. Which is what happens when you choose to do deals with guy like Eddie. You end up in bed with guys like Mr. Elmo. And he's not James Gandalofini. He's not Tony Soprano play-acting tough. I can feel him, across the aisle right now. Looking back at me, laughing. Saying, this ain't got nothing to do with no HBO.

No shit.

Ten years ago I was flying home on this exact same flight. Me and Dad. He'd shown me the ropes around Manila. Introduced me to the oil and gas oligarchs. And I'd gone out on my own and found the last remaining

independent cigar factory in Manila—down from one
hundred and twenty factories in the 1920's.

I dreamed up the whole cigar scheme right there
on the plane. The Splendid Seed Cigar Company,
Double Happiness, Fighting Cock, point of difference,
everything. And Dad was fired up. Man, was he stoked.
We shook on it right then and there. Drank double
bourbons and sang back to back Filipino Baby, just like
when he and Mom got tight.

Thirty minutes out and I'm so screwed. She's not
waking up. My stomach's going crazy.

"Is there something I can get for you before we
land, Mr. Wooten?"

This flight attendant, she's looks very competent.
Like a little Filipina Carly.

"No. I'm fine. Maybe a bottle of water, please."

"My pleasure, Mr. Wooten."

The Laotian chemist said not to drink any water
until thirty minutes out. You get so dried out, he said,
that the balloons seal up in your gut, like a vacuum
pack.

It looks like the flight attendant is wearing a halo
when she hands me the bottle of water. It's a rainbow
halo. It happens sometimes when my contacts get too
dry. "Thank you."

"Good morning, Mrs. Wooten. You've had quite
a nap, haven't you?"

Whiplash does not describe how fast my head just
moved.

"Hey, sweetie," I say, pat-patting her thigh. "How
you feeling?"

"Um, fine, I guess," she says, sitting up and adjusting her cap. "Can I have some water?"

"Sure. Here you go."

"Thanks, sweetie."

I look at her and thank God. She's wearing a halo too, of course.

"You doing okay, sweetie?" she says, patting my hand. "You look a little fucked up."

"No, no. My charmed life continues," I say, flourishing a finger. "I thought you were dead and did a bump. And now you're not and I'm going to throw up."

"How big a bump?"

"Enough to throw up." And then I proceed to do so.

A little bit of vomit squeezes out between my fingers as I lurch down the aisle. But I save the power boot for Mr. Elmo's seat. I'm coating his 40X beaver head with an overdose of Krush. And I've never felt the future so clearly.

"Carly, Carly, check it out," I'm saying, as I crash into the folding bathroom door and then peek back out at all the Asian businessmen trying really hard not to stare at Mr. Elmo's freshly decorated hat.

And Carly's coming up the aisle.

"Baby, check it out," I say, from the floor of an airline toilet.

"I'm dying; I'm lying; I can't quit rhyming."

Okay, wait a minute. Remember what I was saying about telling the truth?

Here's what happened.

None of it.

Some of it, but not the overdosing on heroin part. Or the barfing on Mr. Elmo's hat.

I really did freak, but only in my head. The rest of me executed flawlessly. I guess I still feel like barfing when I think about it—Carly left me for good after that.

She cut a side deal with Mr. Elmo and the Laotian chemist and proceeded to pocket over one million dollars for mule services rendered. Got out undetected, unscathed and her whereabouts remain unknown. Or at least carefully guarded. From me.

No, I was able to pay my father back with the profits from my deal with Mr. Elmo. And I guess the old man will be none too pleased to discover the true source of the payback.

But as the young man, who endured heavy bombing, once said:

"So it goes."

Miss Juicy Owns It

Rockport, Texas
June 19, 2003

His Christian name is Morgan.

His "working" name was Circus Penis.

No joke, gospel truth—hand on the good book.

Of course, Miss Juicy cared less about goofy nicknames. She had a goofy one herself. She just wanted to see for herself. See if all the crazy stories about this Circus Penis dude she heard last night during her shift at ClubPlanet were true. She'd skipped her morning Econ class and headed east on a two-lane blacktop.

And found him pretty quick.

The country where the proud owner of the "Circus" appendage plied his trade was known for duck, deer and quail, bay fishing, shrimping, grain growing, the watching of whooping cranes, and one other thing. Everybody in that part of the world knew what went on behind the door with the red light off Highway 35. And quite a few paid for the privilege.

His secret hustler's lair, his room at the Sea Gun Inn, fit snugly along the edge of Copano Bay and the Aransas Wildlife Refuge—a world of inlets, creeks, and waving blonde grass dotted with motts of trees and razor-thorned bushes—a place where birds came to dance in elaborate rituals.

The Sea Gun's what used to be called a "tourist court." A typical South Texas motel, thirty bucks a pop, oyster shells crunching under tires. A rectangle of rooms surrounding a saltwater swimming pool filled with delighted children during the day and alcoholic adults at night.

Lucky room 7 was a famous place of repose with its red bulb glow, a taste of ocean in the breeze and an interior design shockingly plush. Cinder block walls slathered with latex of the deepest red. Faded sea foam velvet draping the windows and ancient Oriental rugs rumpled on the polished cement floor. An eclectic mix of French Quarter furnishings—fainting couches, benches and slip-covered chairs—nestled around a massive mahogany four-poster. Low light from elegant lamps. Some sweet crooner jazzing on the stereo. A nice hot shower awaiting the aftermath.

He ushered in his seekers with a smile, put his guests at ease with handshakes and kisses on the cheek, set them down to bottles of brown whiskey and cut glass tumblers, nodded to bowls of new age pills and blunts, for those who were so inclined.

And then, without fanfare, he slowly unveiled.

Confident beside his king-size bed, a courtesan's smile playing on his lips, thumbs hooked on loops, pulling the Levi's down. Slowly down.

Oh my god, they said.

Oh my god, they gasped.

Come on, you've got to be kidding.

That thing need a parking permit?

Some, upon making eye contact with the talisman, laughed out loud, or pumped their fists in disbelief, or hopped around the edge of the room, willy-nilly. Some would simply ask for the check. "Check please." And some would stand dumbfounded, mumbling, reaching out to the thing as if drawn by gravitational pull.

Plenty ran out of the room, but most came back, some insisting that all the lights be turned out, to which he would say fine, and pat the sleek sable spread. "Come lay," he would say. And when they did, he whispered to them in a sweet voice. Beautiful, lyrical coos. And soon enough he felt their bodies relax beneath the calming touch of his hands. The room, the lovers, bathed in the blue rays of a 40-inch cathode.

He, mostly, resisted the urge to split the tourists down the middle. The ones who only stared. For them, he would let the sight gag settle in the valley of his well-defined abs, veins throbbing like a flash flood warning. Like swollen blue creeks.

He preferred the greedy fondlers, the glaze in their eyes. And he adored the dainty ones, the seemingly shy. The ones who, inexplicably, wished to take the full measure, the ones who choked and sputtered and coughed, and finally came up for air—looks of pure rapture painted on their faces.

For one and all, he performed. Full service. A full day's pay for a full night's work. And rumors spread, as rumors do, like greasy grassfires. He became famous. Regionally infamous, he liked to say, pointing to the big, tastefully framed map of Texas hanging above the bed. His long elegant finger, tapping the glass, between Corpus and Victoria, where he entertained a Big Top's worth of tricks.

And so it went it for years and years, until she arrived. Under a hurricane warning. Fresh from the City by the Sea, Port Lavaca. Home of the Fighting Sandcrabs.

He would not change her name to Wooten, a pity he could take no wife. Because it was clear that she knew him. That she understood. That she could teach him. This excitable co-ed, this rising senior at Texas A&M-Corpus Christi, deliciously stuffed into a tight T-shirt and low slung jeans. A young woman with unimagined hungers. This, this *explorationist* who marched through his door with unabashed vigor, with powers of articulation the likes of which he had never encountered.

He loved how she used him. To spectacular effect. As if he, alone, was hers.

She did not explain her power over him. She simply undressed and began to displace his control. Pushed him back on the bed. Said nothing.

She had great, good fun with his thing. She shifted it like a trucker going through all fifteen gears. She slapped at it, ground it with her hips. For hours they lounged and cavorted, laughing careless with their seemingly infinite time.

And as the eastern sun rose up the western wall, he felt this new weight press on him, like the heaviest, loveliest problem in the world.

"I'm an accounting major, you know," she said, at ease.

"And of what are you taking into account?" he asked.

"Is that how male prostitutes talk?"

"How do you know I'm a hustler?" he asked. "Maybe I'm falling in love."

"Of course you are," she said, rubbing her thin, inked ankles behind his ears. "Of course you are."

He told her she was enigmatic and profound, which made her pout. He told her she was enigmatic and profound in a good way. In an enigmatic and profound way. He told her he was delighted to make her acquaintance. That she was a most welcome departure from his regular diet of half-starved society matrons, of old money gents, of packs of frat boys and their nicotine strippers who came from every corner of Texas to play.

"Whatever," she said. "You're mine now."

"Really?" he said, most pleased. "To rent or own?"

"Own," she said, smiling the way young girls who look like women can. "As if you didn't know."

And so it went, for weeks and weeks, the spring semester through. The curious couple remained inseparable in spite of schools of haters circling the Sea Gun. Bait fish waiting for the toothsome barracuda to swim away. Whining, scolding, "we want to play!"

But just this minute, Miss Juicy is alone. Alone on a jetty of pink granite that juts far into the Gulf, hair whipping, fists punching the salted gusts of an approaching tropical depression.

She has come to mourn. To lament. To gather strength for her lifeboat rescue.

He told her, before she rushed back for Econ, "It'll only get worse."

She batted luxurious lashes at her unlikely savior, as stately pelicans tilted toward their lanky bodies, framed in the bay front door.

He patiently attempted to explain, to his impatient captor, that the freaks would seek him out. Risk everything for one last slide down the pole.

And this he could not abide. Nor stop.

After so many fleshy, sweaty nights. Hands shaking as the postage-paid key slid into the lock. The laughter of ice cubes hitting the high ball. A shy first hug followed by the acetylene rush to remove clothes. The warp and sump of bodies being plundered.

He could not stop. He lived for their aching, gasping pleasure.

The one true sound in his stormy head.

He had to go away.

"Such a loser!" she cries. Her voice plaintive. His forbidden "love you" ringing in her ears. Wafting around the pink exits of her many piercings. Lingering like the smell of their bed-shared cigars.

She imagines the bittersweet smile on her absent lover's lips.

The cannon fired. Tents folded. The hurdy-gurdy silent.

She can almost taste him. His silly circus penis. Then spits.

She lets no tears. Only raindrops spatter his favorite Juicy blouse.

And then, as the gales howl and the whitecaps froth, she feels a preternatural pull. As if his finger is hooked in the loop of her wide-hipped jeans. Tugging on her like a moon-drenched tide.

Beckoning to her from the shores of an inky black lake. The sad beat of a Mardi Gras dirge lingering in the air.

"I'm so going to kick his ass," she swears.

Marching as to war.

Requiem for a Ten Man

Wickenburg, Arizona
July 25, 2003

Ron, a Ford salesman from Austin, Texas, is explaining, as he sits cross-legged across from Morgan, that prior to the weekend he'd just spent in the Walden Pond detox pen, he'd spent forty-eight hours straight, "smoking rock and selling cars. Selling cars and smoking rock. Sold five Explorer Limiteds to these five little rich fuckers from Dell. Fucking Dellionaires; I mean god bless'em."

As he waits for his new roommate to take a breath, Morgan thinks maybe the guy is still high, but knows better, because the Walden Pond ICU is strict. He's probably just freaked about being in this place.

"Bought me a big ol' loaf of pure," Ron continues, his arms, hands and fingers in subtle, but constant motion. "And I got to smoking and just kept chipping off that loaf until the next thing I know, my wife's calling the paramedics, and the next thing I know they're icing me down in the bathtub to keep my heart from exploding. Hell I don't know. I'm still a little blurry on how I got here. Don't remember a thing about the Austin to Phoenix flight. But here I am."

Morgan sits on the single bed across from Ron, feet on the floor, hands in his lap, trying to commiserate. Trying to understand. He's just finished reading an article in *Rolling Stone* about these guys—white collar crack addicts—and Ron certainly fits the profile—late 20's, maybe early thirties, a nice-looking guy with sandy blonde hair, a little goatee. Short, but muscle-bound strong. Probably make a decent javelin man with a little practice. Good, low center of gravity.

But as Ron continues his dry-drunk rant, Morgan begins to tune out; to ask himself: what the hell? What the hell am *I* doing?"

"Hey, I'm fixing to go for a run," Morgan says, trying to maintain eye contact with his new roommate because it's important not to alienate a peer, especially a new guy.

"A run, dude!" Ron says, still euphoric. "Man, I used to ball all the time down on these outside courts at UT."

"Where? The blue one's across from Memorial Stadium, next to the creek?" says Morgan, seeing the fenced-in sport courts in his mind's eye.

"Exactly dude," Ron says, arching a Belushi-like eyebrow. "How the hell'd you know that?"

"I used to throw javelin on the practice fields next

to those courts."

"No shit," Ron says, scratching at his goatee. "You threw javelin at UT?"

"Naw, not UT," Morgan says, not really wanting to get into it. "Little school called Permian A&I. Division II, no big deal."

"Odessa Permian, man that's some bad-ass football in that town," Ron says, stretching his arms over his head, flexing his biceps, but not in a show-off way.

Morgan, for the first time in his life, doesn't want to talk sports. He doesn't want to patiently explain to his new roommate that Odessa Permian is a high school, and yeah, they do play good football, but I went to Permian A&I and I'm a decathlete, not just a javelin guy, and who gives a damn anyway. Nobody gives a damn whether we're car salesmen or decathletes or the It Girl in London, or a political consultant from Detroit, or a publisher from Manhattan, or a gay playwright from Chicago, or a housewife from Phoenix, or the son of a broccoli magnate from San Jose, or a nuclear physicist from White Sands.

This is what Morgan's brain does in this place, he thinks, runs a hundred miles an hour, no attention, no retention; running on nothing but crappy decaf and hours and hours of yakking and listening, yakking and listening about your own and everybody else's screwed up life.

"Hey you okay?" Ron asks.

"Yeah, fine. Sorry," Morgan says, then leans forward into a calf stretch. "Place kind of make me space out a lot."

"I can believe that," Ron says, unfolding his

pretzel legs, then stretching out on the bed.

Morgan switches his calf stretch. Smiles when Ron closes his eyes and exhales a deep sigh.

"So you cool?" says Morgan, feeling his calf muscle cramp, flutter involuntarily, then finally relax. "You doing okay?"

"Yeah, man; I'm cool," Ron says. "You know, buggin' big time. And tired as hell, man. Seems like I've been up for the past three years."

"You probably have," Morgan says. "Me too. Probably can't qualify for this place without at least a couple of sleepless years."

"No doubt."

"All right, I'm gone," Morgan says, reaching to shake Ron's hand.

"Have a good one," says the new roommate, giving Morgan a soul shake, then webbing his fingers behind his head.

"Listen, you're in the right place," Morgan says as he opens the door to their room. "It may not feel like it right now, but you'll do it. You'll be all right."

"Hope so, man," Ron says, opening his eyes. "Sure do hope so. Got to."

As he walks slowly away from the dormitory, along the sidewalks, through the tightly clustered ranch style buildings, Morgan nods to the new people whose names he hasn't learned, and greets, by name, the few counselors and patients he knows. He hasn't run in over six, maybe eight months, and while he hates that he's let himself get this out of shape, he's excited about the hup-two-three-four; the mindless shuffle of the slow jog.

He stops alongside the sand volleyball court and double ties his shoelaces. He notices a newbie, sitting in the shade of a giant saguaro cactus, drawing a smiley face on a volleyball. He heard from the It girl that this one's a cutter. And sure enough, he sees the telltale striations, the angry purple keloid scars running up the young girl's bare arms. He'd like to say something to her, when she looks up at him. Anything—compliment her Nebraska Cornhusker T-shirt, the purple rinse in her auburn hair—but can only wave.

Morgan is grateful when she lifts her hand and mouths, "Hi."

"Afternoon," he says, undecided about his next step. "Desert treating you okay?"

She looks up at him, combs her fingers through the long hair hanging in front of her face, flips it back dramatically. "Yeah, kinda," she says. "It's so hot."

Back in his flirting days Morgan would have come closer; attempted the clever line, calculated the possibility. He wants those days to be over; needs to be straight with this fellow seeker. "Yeah, us fair-skinned folks have to be careful," he says, careful to keep moving. "See ya."

He heads out of the compound and steps on to the gravel road that runs below the bluff where the campus sits. He starts walking, then slowly jogging, down into Walden Pond's acres of undeveloped Sonora Desert.

The ground looks moonscapish; rocks and boulders in varying shades of grey and white on either side of the graded slash of road; everything bleached except for the occasional green of a low cactus, or the tiny orange or yellow bloom. The sun glows hazy white in a cloudless sky, blazing listlessly at four-o'clock. The heat rises in waves off the ground, oven-like, but for once, Morgan isn't sweating from the second he steps outside. He likes what thirty-two days of sobriety has done for his body. His muscles are beginning to reappear after months of hibernation beneath beer carbs and munchy fat. He doesn't want to be "ripped" again—that's young man's vanity, but being fit; being able to run three miles, that'll be nice.

I'm still only three years out from being a world-class decath…

Fuck that, just run. Just shut up and run.

And so he does. Easily down a hill and on to the wide riverbed plain, where flash floods are said to rage on the rare occasion rain actually makes it to the ground.

Slow, he tells himself. Slow, slow the hell down. No stopwatch, just nice and easy. No sixty second quarters. Hell, walk if you want. Relax, heel toe, heel toe, shake it out a little; loosen up. There you go; just a little mid-afternoon *vuelta* through the pretty pipe cactus; nice sun, beautiful heat. Crack your neck; it's cool, crack it all up.

As Morgan puts half a mile's distance down the unmarked road, his exit interview, from earlier in the morning, comes to mind. It was a particularly intense session with the man who started Walden Pond, Dr. Julius Millard.

"Blissful ignorance is not an option," he had told the good doctor. "And if I do backslide, there's an excellent chance that I'll be incarcerated, or die, or both."

"Mr. Wooten," Dr. Millard said, closing a manila file folder. "Let me assure you that dying is the least of your worries. You're young, healthy and strong. Living in the present, in reality. One day at a time is where you must focus. "

"Yes sir, Dr. Millard," Morgan said, looking the man in the eye and holding his gaze steady. "I understand what you're saying."

He remembers Dr. Millard's head nodding in agreement and saying finally: "And do you understand, that telling people, especially people you perceive to be in authority, telling these authority figures what they want to hear is *the* hallmark of the sociopathetic personality?"

Morgan remembers almost laughing, marveling at the consistency of every single one of these doctors and counselors; how lockstep and devoted they all were.

"Absolutely," he'd answered. "That's going to be my biggest challenge: Telling the truth."

"Okay then, Mr. Wooten," Dr. Millard said, standing in front of his enormous, paper-crammed desk. "I think you've done some fine, hard work here. And you must always remember that Walden Pond is here to help you overcome your anxieties, every day, even after you leave our campus. Just remember, only *you* know if you're being honest. Only *you* can heal yourself. It's a daunting task."

"I'm up to it, Dr. Millard," he'd said. "I really am."

Morgan is at end of the graded road, but his breathing is still relaxed, and he's barely broken a sweat. He looks back at the compound, maybe a mile and half away, and decides to do a little sand work in the riverbed.

He needs to put a little more distance between himself and his good-intentioned healers; needs more than a little respite from the ultra-earnest specialists.

He wants to conjure, instead, for just a bit, a plan to win back the crazy girl from Port Lavaca—the Fighting Sandcrab. Meeting her had been such a frightening stroke of good fortune. She was the closest thing to Carly that he'd met since those smoke-filled days in the Philippines.

But...he thinks, high stepping across rippled waves of sand that swallow his cross-trainers...it is, what it is.

It is what it is. And it's high time to get over it. You're not a decathlete, you're not some red-bulb hustler living by the bay. You're Morgan Wooten, dude. And all it's time to do is find your girl, coach some kids, and reacquaint yourself with...

Sidewinders.

At dawn the next day, a Walden Pond search party found a pair of the native pit vipers guarding Morgan Wooten's fetally-positioned body.

A somber counselor said, as they gathered around the peaceful sleeper, that the snakes were probably attracted to his body heat.

But the young woman, dressed in immaculate

white, could not explain why the snakes still lingered with Morgan after sunrise.

As if Morgan and the sidewinders were communing.

As if they were exchanging notes; on next steps.

Peace of Mind

Saint John The Baptist Parish, Louisiana
February 28, 2005

Just a while back, I was driving home from a Society of Civil Engineers conference in Mobile, Alabama; hands at ten and two, wheeling my four-door Buick down the old concrete ribbon. The morning was a dewdrop sunny spring and I was drinking my breakfast beverage of choice—Community Coffee with a splash of Pet milk.

As an expert trained in stress and load-bearing management, I could not get over the structural integrity of our Interstate System. The jaunty smile in my rearview pretty much said it all: Our life and times were simply magical.

I pulled off at a truck stop with easy access in Pass Christian, Mississippi to call my wife. She told me the marriage was over and that she was running away with Mark Spitz. I told her…actually I don't remember what I said, except she wouldn't get very far, and then hung up.

I was shocked. No doubt about it—thirteen years of marriage to a central Texas society gal. Living comfortably in Albuquerque, in a tasteful adobe ranch style, with thick pile carpet and a devastating view of the Zuni Mountains—she flushed it all, in less than thirty seconds.

I had to ask, "What in the H-E-Double Toothpicks?"

I stomped around the parking lot. Not much caring who saw what. At least until a rail-thin trucker in a Southern Miss hat offered me a slice off his plug.

I told him, right then and there. I said, "Hey, man, this is no time for tobacco." The trucker cut his eyes at me, folded his lockblade, pocketed his plug. "Hell you say, mister."

He was right about that. At least the me being in Hell part. I buckled up, popped a Tums, and merged with traffic. It was a long way to Albuquerque—plenty of time to work things out.

In no time at all, I was deep inside the load-bearing ability of my wife's exceptionally wide beam. I giddily contemplated the G-forces involved in every satisfying swat of a freshly cut birch against her quivering buttocks, but then quickly reconsidered.

I said, "Be cool, man—corporal punishment fantasies? What's up with that?"

But boy was I fuming. "Running off with Mark Spitz. I mean, what the hell?"

I floored it—made that Buick scream.

On the outskirts of Slidell, a young trooper, with a neatly trimmed mustache, pulled me over for excessive speed. At that moment, I thought he vaguely resembled a certain famous Olympic swimmer from the 70s.

When I handed him my driver's license I made the mistake of brushing some dandruff onto his clipboard. Officer Huckleby looked embarrassed, then mad, when the roller on his ballpoint clogged.

"It's my wife's fault," I said.

"What's your wife's fault?"

"Nervous exfoliation."

"Sir," said the trooper, calmly capping his pen. "I'm going to need you to step out of the car, please."

"Yes sir," I replied, quickly unbuckling.

He asked me to perform a series of multi-task coordination drills, all of which I passed without error. After my ability to recite the alphabet backward was rigorously confirmed, the trooper's expression turned quizzical, then intense. "Sir," he said, removing his aviator sunglasses. "How would you characterize your mental status?"

Not the expected query, but I charged ahead, unabashed. "Good," I said, attempting the chipper tone. "I'm doing much better, thank you."

"Much better than when?"

"Than when my wife calmly told me that she was leaving me for Mark Spitz—the seven-time Olympic gold medalist swimmer."

"Oh," said Officer Huckleby, lifting the brim of his trooper's hat ever so slightly with the tip of his clogged pen. "Mr. Wooten, I need you to reenter your vehicle and wait for further instructions."

"Yes sir," I said, smiling. "Anybody ever confuse you for Mark Spitz?"

"No sir. You're the first," he said, gesturing to my car door. "Have a seat, Mr. Wooten. "

To say I was shocked by Officer Huckleby's subsequent display of compassion is an understatement. In fact, the curious circumstances that allowed me to receive a warning, rather than pay a $163 fine, lifted my spirits clear across the breadth of the Pelican State.

But optimism fatigue set in when I hit the business loop in Beaumont. I remembered my wife had Mark Spitz's famous poster hanging in her dorm room at Eastern New Mexico State. Seven gold medals in '72. You don't see mustaches like that on swimmers any more.

I was still fighting the jealous current, flowing out of Portales, when I passed the City of Houston Sewage Treatment Plant.

Spitz is past his prime, I thought. He used to be a helluva stud, breaking all those world records. Hell, breaking all those hearts.

I envisioned my wife, in a racy new lingerie ensemble, watching a DVD of his legendary exploits. I could hear her mouthing sweet nothings to him by the light of our Sony WEGA. "Mark, I've got something warm to towel off with" ("Okay honey, right after I sign the endorsement contract").

I rolled down the window and stuck my head out into the slipstream. The air was thick with the smell of petroleum by-products. As I drove across the glorious

Houston Ship Channel Bridge, with its expansive view of the world's largest contiguous refining and petro-chemical complex, I finally figured it out.

I had to pick up a hitchhiker.

And sure enough, there he was. Big guy. Leaning up against the perimeter fence of the Budweiser brewery, just inside the Houston city limits.

He entered my vehicle with thanks and praise and quickly pulled a sleeve of amphetamines from his New England Patriots duffel. I offered him a drink. And after washing down three tablets with a foamy pull off my Lone Star quart, he offered to drive. Seconds later, I buckled up, stuck my leg out the passenger window, and off we went.

In no time, the hitchhiker zoomed us clear to the base of the Llano Estacado.

Big guy turned out to be a former football star for the Angelo State Rams. So good, in fact, that he continued his crushing ways as a linebacker with the Patriots, which answered my duffel bag question. He said he had head-butted some of the best—from Earl Campbell to Emmitt Smith. He went on to explain that he was now nothing but a fat happy family man. Married to a girl he met at Mass in Foxborough. And that they'd had two girls. And recently, a newborn son.

My thick-necked driver, with an equally thick wal-rus mustache, told me he'd been so overwhelmed by his son's arrival that he rushed out of the hospital and drove straight to the San Jacinto Monument. To give thanks.

I had to admit, it was a disturbing testimonial, but I plunged ahead, open to suggestion.

He said the reason he was hitchhiking was because he donated his car to a family in Friendswood whose son was killed during Spring Break by dope people in Matamoras. He said he'd finished with his newborn's halleluiahs at the San Jacinto Monument (I didn't ask) and was drinking a cup of coffee with his jelly-filled at the local Shipley's Do-Nuts, when he read the story about the Friendswood quarterback done bad. He said he left his car in care of the Shipley's manager.

And you can bet I was doing a little praying to Jesus myself at that point.

"My boy was born, and these people had just lost their son," the big guy testified, as we navigated through the central Texas sagebrush. "I gave'em my car."

"Absolutely," I nodded sagely. "And now you're driving us to the promised land at a high rate of speed."

"On the wings of angels. Me and you, captain. Winging it," he said, then removed his wrap-around sunglasses and delivered my second look of compassion in less than twenty-four hours.

I asked how was it he could drive from the Beaumont-side of Houston, all the way to Eden, before the sun went down. "I used to chew uppers like Grape-Nuts when I was playing ball." he offered. "Laser focus, my man. Ain't it something."

"*Vaya con dios,*" said the big guy, leaning into the passenger-side window as I turned the ignition. Clamped to his broad shoulders were two radiant teenage daughters, who glowingly said, "we're cheerleaders."

I could only imagine as the big guy's daughters completed crisp tumbling routines, while, just beyond the carpet grass, Mama and baby rocked on the porch. They all—this handsome nuclear family—looked positively dreamy to me.

So, how to describe a flat-out, two-lane pilgrimage with the big guy?

Let's just say that listening to the former linebacker allowed me to put my own personal dilemmas into perspective. My chance encounter with the highly animated acolyte led me to believe that the stress and load bearing of life-changing events manifests itself in strange ways.

After delivering my celestial load, heretofore unknown options began to reveal themselves during a hard, solo, dead-of-the-night drive from the banks of the Concho River to New Mexico.

A plump prostitute in Big Spring tempted me, but I opted for salty coffee at the 7-Eleven instead.

I stretched my legs in Clovis; pitched some fifty-cent pieces with a roadside fruit vendor in the cool morning breeze. "My wife wants what she wants," I said, counting the silver Kennedys in my over-caffeinated palms. "And it ain't happening on forty grand a year—even with the occasional kickback."

"Double or nothing for the radar detector?" asked the enterprising citrus slinger. I'd already taken the teen, who sported a beautiful wisp of a mustache, for $3.50. I told him, "I'll gladly trade my radar for a bag of your sweet Valley oranges." Obviously not the deal the young man expected from a gringo as we exchanged knowing glances along with our material goods.

Later that morning, I pulled into Albuquerque and headed straight for the Country Club. I sat and drank Mount Gay and the juice of oranges freshly squeezed by my favorite peppy waitress from Ho Chi Minh City. She said, "boat people very happy," then plucked a thread of lavender silk from her traditional *ao dai* dress.

Frankly, I had my doubts about boat people or any people being happy. But I matched her toothy grin and signed my father-in-law's name for the last time. I pondered next steps, all my options.

That night I decided to be a truck driver.

Just as impulsively as the Patriot linebacker had given up his car, I gave up my plush existence in the valley of the Zuni Mountains; and the woman who was my wife. If she was determined to chase glory with Mark Spitz, with a man in a star-spangled Speedo, then so be it. All I wanted was fifteen tons in the back of my Peterbilt.

Post-Curveball, I was a truck driver. You know big forearms, hazard to your health. Scared the crap out of foreign compacts. No CB radio and no hitchhikers. Liked my driving lonely. CDL licensed. Albuquerque to Pensacola. Two years straight. Forgot all about Santa Fe and blue corn tortillas with organic salsa.

I picked up my load Monday afternoon. Hit the road early Tuesday morning. Slept in Beaumont on Wednesday. Reloaded in Pensacola on Thursday. Back in Albuquerque for the weekend. A real man of the road in the finest 8-track, mutton-chop tradition.

Eventually, I met a truckstop waitress in Beaumont and stayed at her place during the week. Jessica's the one who told me about the Make Mine A Double Club. Her Aunt Jolene had just opened it on the I-55 Bridge between Manchac and Hammond. She said it was an orange building on the eastbound right-of-way. Smack in the middle of Honey Island Swamp.

I said, "I'll be damned. A bar on a bridge."

I liked this girl from Beaumont. Jessica was a fine woman. Always had a cold Lone Star and pan-fried liver waiting for me, Tuesday for supper and Thursday for lunch. She even made me brush my teeth before we went to bed. I think we made a decent pair. A couple the Gallup Poll might be interested in.

But our fortunes changed on a Fat Tuesday night. And I should have seen it coming.

I pulled into Beaumont right on time. I could tell Jessica had enjoyed the last day of Mardi Gras. The daiquiris smelled sweet on her breath. I thought she might be up for a steak, or some Chinese. A little liver relief.

"I eat liver because my blood's iron-poor," she said, stabbing two thin-sliced pieces from her well-seasoned pan, then slapped them on my plate.

I took a swig of cold Lone Star.

"Take some Geritol," I said.

But that's all it took.

"I need you to leave."

Not what I expected from a gal so seemingly smitten. But like I said, Jessica was a fine woman, and her pride was intact when I exited her back door for the final time. With 157 plates of liver lodged in my colon.

I hit the road; tried my best to feel reborn, but the interruption in routine disturbed me. I was depressed.

The moon was out, but the highway felt dead. Just as I was reaching for my aspirin bottle, I passed a sign for I-55 North. I followed the directions blindly, across misty bogs and foggy bayous, for what seemed like a long time. But then, there it was—the gleaming white beauty of the I-55 Bridge.

I got the same kind of feeling I had right before I shot the last free throw at the Regional Finals. Tingling, queasy excitement.

And not sixty seconds later I caught a burning patch of color in the high beams, a screaming-nightmare-safety orange. I geared her down and nudged my 120 feet of rig against the guardrail.

I got down out of the cab, walked over, and slapped a cinder block. Ran my hand over the thick fresh paint. "The Make Mine A Double Club." I said it out loud.

"That's what it is. Come on in. I'm Sid," he said, extending a handful of stumpy digits. We shook, and gave each other the once over. He was a fun-bellied guy, about five cinder blocks tall, dressed in red coveralls with flames stitched on the butt. He was wearing an Abbousie Hardware baseball cap up high on his crew-cut skull.

It was dark inside when we walked through the screen door of the bar. I stared at a lit-up "Occupied" sign behind the bar while Sid set up two shot glasses. Beer-sign neon from Dixie, Falstaff and Jax provided the only light. Sid took off his cap, threw a ringer on a nail to his left, and said, "I serve an honest drink and this establishment holds three people. You, me and Sheriff Jolene. But don't mistake me for the bartender. I've seen a lot of men serving highballs in white cotton gloves."

I nodded yes, but to be honest, I was thinking about pan-fried liver and why the hell I wasn't still a civil engineer. Honestly spacing out. Then I heard the slap of skin on fiberglass, and water rushing through pipes, and a kind of low moan gurgling behind the Occupied sign and I began wondering just what in the...

"Now listen here," Sid said, ignoring the racket behind the bar. "Sheriff Jolene Aboussie is living testimony to the power of stretch fabrics. Looks like Shelley Winters in her prime. She's got a gold poly law enforcement outfit that is directly responsible for this bridge. Twenty-five miles of divided, elevated, reinforced concrete four-lane Interstate running the length of Saint John The Baptist Parish. She put us on the map, son."

"She's a beauty," I agreed. The load bearing capacity of the bridge had to be tremendous.

He poured two shots of cloudy liquor and shook out a dash of Tabasco in each. All I could think was "violent discharge" after I swallowed. Eyes watering. Mouth wide open. But Sid didn't flinch, squint or holler.

I took courage.

"Those TV preacher boys think they've got their finger on the money line," he went on, retrieving my glass. "But Jolene Abboussie can show'em how to ladle some cash. I'd say this bridge ranks right up there with the Tombigbee Waterway. Pork barrel deluxe."

By now, things had settled down considerably behind the Occupied sign. So I took a seat. Stopped thinking about pan fried liver and let my instincts take over. Seemed important.

Sid said, "but ever since Jolene dedicated that bottle of sour mash upside the guard rail of this fine span, she wanted to build a proper drinking establishment. She's been trying to get one of those man-made island turnarounds built, like the one midway down the Atchafalaya Bridge. But it's a patience game. She's got a new MiracleKnit jumpsuit that would get the ball rolling during good times, but the lobbyists say that until OPEC gets the price of oil up to a hundred, even a personal visit from Jolene won't bankroll that project."

I have to believe my eyes were glazing, but Sid was on a roll.

"So in the mean time, she built The Make Mine A Double here on the bridge shoulder and asked me to run it. She used it as a duck blind for the first two seasons. Then she knocked out the guardrail and installed a kitchenette and a bunk out over the water for me. The bathroom's right there. It's one of those commercial airline toilets. Same principle; empties right into the swamp. Peggy's in there now."

"Who?"

"Your new girlfriend, Peggy," Sid said, and shot me a wink. "She keeps her skiff tied down below on the superstructure. Makes her own rope ladder out of hemp."

"I bet."

Sid ignored that, and threw some popcorn in the microwave, then went looking for something under the bar.

I was feeling better. Even a little excited about this new girlfriend. "I used to do a little bridge building myself," I said. "Used to be civil engineer, but now I drive for W&L."

Sid responded with a flat-footed nip-up to the bar and sang, "WHO-WEEE! Pig on the griddle. Fat night, I'm in the middle. Eat bite fuck suck gobble nibble chew. My gut's burning, how 'bout you?"

Boy! I started feeling kind of partyish. Let out a WHOOP! of my own, watching Sid hoof on that bar.

"Sheriff Jolene says Peggy's a swamp girl. But I tell you what I think," Sid said, still beating the soft-shoe. "I think somebody took every shade of gold and brown in the world and lots of that Frenchy tanning oil. I think they threw it all in a paint mixer down at the Hardware, let it shake for twenty four, then dipped that girl in it."

"Damn, Sid!" I said, practically yelling. "Can I meet her?"

He laced his fingers just right and blew a righteous duck call. "Peggy! We got a live one." then hopped down from the bar, looked me in the eye, and said,

"How 'bout another shot?"

"Why not," I said, hoping for the best.

And as I swallowed the cloudy liquid, Peggy came out of the toilet in a floor-length figure-huggin'dress made of large shimmering sequins. She was handling something long and flexible, but I couldn't make it out; my eyes were watering bad from the whiskey.

Then I heard Sid giggling and Peggy chanting:

"Red touching yella, dangerous fella; red touching yella, dangerous fella."

I fell back against the far wall, dizzy, jaws wide open, and damn if she didn't feed that thing right into my mouth. Chewed on me pretty good, too.

I guess. Damn snakes.

All I remember was Sid turning off the beer neon and closing the door behind him. Then Peggy putting me over her shoulder and carrying me down the hemp ladder to her own personal pirogue.

She started paddling us across Lake Maurepas, mopping my fevered brow with her long black hair. Her sequins glowed like mother-of-pearl. I sat up and watched Mark Spitz butterflying down the bayou. It's so beautiful. He was like this huge manta ray; half-submerged, half-flying through that smooth black water.

And for a moment...I feel it...muscles soft... whirlywheeliewowing in that velvety dark. "Peace of....

Three days later Sheriff Jolene dragged Peggy and me out of the mudbug muck. Then she threw us one helluva cremation. Sid hired a band of puffy cheeked sax boys to blow while our pelvic girdles smoldered in the creamy pink light of dawn. Everybody swaying and a singing, "come-a, gonna carry me home."

Sheriff Jolene still throws the annual I-55 Bridge Tournament and Coral Snake Extravaganza, in our honor. Last year Bill Gates and Warren Buffet showed up and bet more money than God. In fact, Sid skimmed enough of the profits to mount solid brass busts of Peggy and me on top of the airline toilet.

Which is quite a tribute, considering.

So hey, hey pocky way; you beginning to get the picture?

That's cool.

It's not about Mark Spitz and the missus K-I-S-S-I-N-G. Or divorce attorneys barking up my tree.

It's not about evangelical linebackers fried to the core. Or a Beaumont beauty trying to even the score.

Think about a snake-handling maiden with corn on the side. And your old gone trucker eyeing the prize.

Think about me, and Peggy, and peace of mind.

Charles Alcorn was born and raised in Victoria on the Coastal Bend of Texas. He graduated with a BA in Geology from Washington & Lee University, where he also played linebacker and threw the javelin and discus for the Generals. He received his MA in English from the University of Southern Mississippi's Center for Writers and his PhD in Creative Writing/English Literature from the University of Houston's Creative Writing Program.

Alcorn currently serves on the faculty of the University of Houston-Victoria and is the Managing Editor of the *American Book Review*. His area of academic interest includes a hybrid genre—Gothic Realism—that draws from the Magic Realism of Gabriel García Márquez and Carlos Fuentes, the American road of mysticism of Jack Kerouac and the Beats as well as the Southern/Southwest Realism of late twentieth-century writers such as Larry McMurtry, Barry Hannah, and Antonya Nelson.

He currently splits teaching assignments between the UH campuses in Sugar Land and Victoria. He lives in mid-town Houston with wife Angela and two sons.